Yorkshire Pudding

Love is a destination

Stacy Erin Myers

Yorkshire Pudding

Love is a destination

Stacy Erin Myers

Love, it seems, is transcendental. At least that's what Monique ("Momo") and nine-year-old Tutor Moot think after discovering beautiful and serendipitous connections between their herd of Yorkshire terriers that they breed and sell, and the people the little terriers choose as their owners. A comforting tale of life lessons, everlasting love, and evidence that nothing is ever happenstance, *Yorkshire Pudding*, set in 1969, is the year in a life of a mother-daughter duo that discovers their unique bond—both personally and through struggles of the era. Momo and Tutor together learn about themselves, their community, and society's discriminations.

Yorkshire Pudding not only invites readers into the lives of a single eccentric mother and her precocious daughter, but also into the lives of a handful of very diverse neighbors, all of whom are changed forever when the Moot puppies come into their lives. Having lost her husband while pregnant with Tutor, Momo tries desperately to create a family for her expectant child. The dog breeding business has a lot more to offer than income, she soon finds out, as the loving disposition of their Yorkshire terriers fills the void of loss.

A small neighborhood is the backdrop for six people longing for a second chance at life, happiness, and perhaps a little closure. When fate intervenes, each of them finds that an unexpected gift can be found in a most unusual reincarnated package, as a little puppy.

Yorkshire Pudding serves up a whimsical, celestial tale that will resonate with any reader who has ever loved a dog. Big on inspiration, this heavenly little story will melt the heart and bring sweet tears to the eyes of anyone who believes that dogs do smile and have souls—and it will make you smile the next time you see a dog wag its tail.

***

This is a work of fiction. The events described are imaginary,
and the characters are fictitious and not
intended to represent specific living persons.

Myers, Stacy E.
Yorkshire Pudding / Stacy Erin Myers

ISBN# 1-929845-51-0
First Title
The text of this book is set in Times New Roman.
Cover and text design by: Mike Bowman

Published by DeFranco Entertainment

To my love Tony, for giving me back
the sweetest part of my childhood,
the gift of Tahlulah.

Ever has it been that love knows
not its own depth until the hour of separation.

Kahili Gibran

Table Of Contents

Moot Point
June 2011

One
June 2010

Two
432 West Denslow Avenue, 1969

Three
Bon Ton

Four
Monique and Raleigh

Five
Moot Love, 1958-1959

Six
Mrs. Van Steenkiste, Spring 1969

Seven
Scooter Pie

Eight
Mr. Early

Nine
Crumpet

Ten
HedyMae and Charles, 1937

Eleven
"Niche"

Twelve
Whiskey

Thirteen
Scooter Pie, Summer 1969

Fourteen
Pudding

Fifteen
Miss Kimura

Sixteen
Momo Knows Best

Seventeen
The Connections, June 2011

About the Author

If a dog will not go home with you after looking you in the face,
you should go home and examine your conscience.
- Woodrow Wilson

Moot Point

June 2011

Certain aromas take me back in time, triggering emotions like nothing else. The smell of honeysuckle, or the scent of vert green grass freshly cut after the evening dew has nourished it. And fragrant summer evenings, like tonight, that linger with orange blossom and lavender that beckons me to crank open my old kitchen window and breathe it all in.

A warm breeze pushes on the wind chimes that hang from the eighty-year-old apricot tree in our front yard; weathered and splintered, its dry old broken bark still pops with youthful pink flowers. The scent of our wisteria washes over the front porch eave and evokes memories of my childhood, as does the concoction I'm baking tonight that fills my kitchen and my mind with the smell of rosemary, pulling me further backward to that special year when I was nine years old and anything seemed possible.

It was one short year, yet it was an impressionable year, and a time I still cherish. As I stand at my kitchen sink and watch the neighborhood streetlights flicker on, I start to ruminate. I slowly wash and inspect my aged hands and I think about how I used to think that the frogs in Miss Kimura's pond could give me warts. The thought makes me smile now. I remember when my mother came up with an idea for removing warts. She was creative when it came to remedies: a simple lemon rind soaked in red wine vinegar and a dash of salt; marinate for one day and then cut to the exact size of the wart, bandage tight, and leave alone overnight. When the bandage was removed the next morning she would slice the pickled wart right off with a razor blade and no more frog wart! I smile again and sip my jammy Malbec that smells like figs and HedyMae's fruit pie specials.

I was exposed to a lot of new things in 1969, back in my small world, experiencing my fair share of so-called happenstances. But now, as I dry my hands and glance around my kitchen floor at my five sleeping dogs, I can't help but find the irony in it all. I like to bake at night, taking my time, sipping wine while making up culinary experiments of my own. My dogs, scattered around the kitchen, nostrils twitching, patiently wait for their bite to be tossed to the floor, but it's my Yorkie who is my harshest and fondest food critic. She sits by herself, almost under my foot, staring straight up, tongue slightly out, eyes blinking.

Tonight I open the oven and carve off a small slice of what will be tonight's dinner. The sweet-smelling heat sweeps over my face and I know it will be delicious. As I let the bite cool on the fork, my Yorkie starts to wiggle her tail end with impatience. The other dogs watch this without interrupting, as they know the routine. My Yorkie opens her mouth and slowly pulls the meat off the fork and chews, slowly, almost thoughtfully, then looks up with ears pinned to her head, eyes half-shut, her tail wagging. I've passed the taste test once again and I think of my mother and how it's been just a year since I received this little dog and the connection to my mother that came with her.

One

Over the years I've had my romances and heartbreaks. But true love, in its natural, pure form, has always eluded me, so I've worked too hard. After my mother died, when I was thirty, I kept the restaurant she co-owned with her dear friend HedyMae. I kept it going for almost ten years, unchanged, because why change what works? This is what I told myself anyway, until one day I just became too tired. My hands hurt from years of work. I was fifteen when I started working at the restaurant and forty when I stopped. I think I was talked out, baked out, and worn out, and I just didn't care about filling up the pies or the time anymore.

I sold the restaurant and its brand, "Niche," after I was able to make some money by selling my own brand of frozen food products, allowing me to stop working. I stopped doing anything work-related, actually, and started taking long hikes, quiet walks on the beach, and drives along the coast with no particular destination. I found myself a little rescue mutt to join me on my wanderings, to keep me company and to listen to me talk. Then I got another. They were the best listeners and the most loyal dogs I could wish for. I loved them more than anything, as they were my only family—and they in turn loved me more than unconditionally. They were my guardians for a while. I had them well into my marriage, a marriage that came late in life.

I was almost forty-two when my husband found me one late afternoon sitting atop a sand dune watching my dogs trying to run down the seagulls and the sandpipers along the shore. I applauded their efforts. It was a day when you could almost imagine hearing the sun sizzle as it sank into the cold ocean water. Years have passed since that perfect day we met, and now we've been happily married for almost eight years. We never focused on having children. If it happened, wonderful, and if not, well, living on an acre with a few horses, cats, chickens, rabbits, birds, and five dogs is fine, too. Three of those dogs were his when we met—and the fact that he had so many dogs was one of the many reasons he was perfect for me. We had a big happy animal family, which was a very complete family as far as I was concerned.

I never had the baby craving—maybe because I grew up without siblings, surrounded by dogs as my playmates. It never really crossed my mind how unusual my childhood was until one recent evening when I was cooking dinner with all our dogs present. There was one in each corner of the kitchen, and my little Chihuahua, Pixy Stick, was at my feet. I suddenly felt the back of my neck tingle and I looked over at my husband. He was sipping tequila and thumbing through a cookbook when his phone rang. What followed was a short conversation that required him to go out to attend to one of his clients. This client needed to sign some documents he had overlooked, and my husband said he would be back in about an hour.

The familiarity of the scenario that night was undeniable. It was like déjà-vu, only what had unfolded was something I hadn't actually experienced firsthand. My husband, sitting at the kitchen table, was the image of Raleigh, sitting as he often did, admiring my mother while she made her Yorkshire pudding. I looked around our kitchen and the hair stood high on my forearm. I felt another strange feeling. I wrapped my arms around my husband and smelled his neck. I kissed it and told him to not be too long, that I was making a delicious concoction. He stared into my eyes for a second and smiled, kissed me on the lips then smacked his lips and said, just before leaving, "I taste braised short ribs!"

I poured a little wine, and then just a little more, and sat on the kitchen floor and called my dogs to gather around. They sleepily obeyed, wagging their tails, and sat to listen to me talk about the Yorkies we had back when I was a child. Those Yorkies were still close to my heart after all these years, and my poor husband had heard a million tales about my childhood, the dogs, Momo and Raleigh, and all the kismets that occurred in 1969. Whenever I finished nostalgic reminiscing, he'd always asked the same exasperated question, "Why not get another Yorkie? Stop torturing yourself." But I couldn't. It just wouldn't be the same without my mother; it wouldn't be one of the Moot dogs, and I just didn't believe I could ever have a dog like HoneyWest again.

And that would be the beginning and the end of a conversation we'd have every few months. But that night was different. It was June, the day before my mother's birthday, and I explained to my dogs that maybe the reason I felt so strange was because I was feeling a little melancholy. I lightly ran my hand over each dog's head and gently tugged on an ear or a tail to lighten my mood. Then I went back to making my concoction that simmered on the stove; the smell of rosemary and figs filled the air.

My husband sells real estate, and was in the middle of an escrow. The client who had called, the one who needed to sign some more papers, happened to be a famous actor and father to a teenage daughter who was moving back east, promptly. As my husband relayed the story to me, the client was a single father with a very rebellious, spoiled daughter. He desperately wanted to get her out of Los Angeles and thought the East Coast would be a better environment for her. Apparently, the private Catholic girls school she attended was only making matters worse, with drugs and superficial competition making up the core of her after-school curriculum.

The last straw snapped recently when his daughter was in yet another car accident, this time in the middle of the night. She smashed into a neighbor's mailbox, hitting her head on the steering wheel so hard she was hospitalized for a week. The effort of keeping the juicy situation quiet from the gossip girls, as well as the gossip columnists, was just too laborious; better to just leave town. While recuperating from her head trauma, the daughter managed to escape from the hospital. Dressed only in her robe, she called a friend and left in the middle of the night. She disappeared for a few days and holed up with a few bad influences. She went on a shopping spree with cash she withdrew from an ATM minutes after her escape. Her spending romp in Beverly Hills cost her father ten thousand dollars.

"Not too bad," her father told my husband nonchalantly, flashing his famous smile. "She just misses her mother," he rationalized. "She died last year and I'm not around much for my daughter these days because of my crazy location shoots."

What turned out to mostly perturb him was that his daughter had purchased a four-month-old puppy that she'd tossed aside as if it were a fashion accessory.

Along with the dog, she'd bought a few rhinestone collars, leashes, rhinestone sweaters, at least twenty toys, and a rhinestone doggy tote bag—but no food. Then she'd hidden the puppy, for God knows how long, until its whimpers turned into howls and the housekeeper found it tangled up in dirty clothes in the back of the teenager's closet.

"The fact that my daughter neglected the puppy worries me," he told my husband. "She might be trying to tell me something. What do you think?" My husband thought his client's daughter was a spoiled brat, but kept that to himself.

The night he went to his client's house to finish up the paperwork turned out to be a night that would change our lives, because the client, as fate would have it, needed to ask my husband for a favor.

***

One of my pleasures in life is cooking, and being in my kitchen cooking with all my dogs sitting around keeping me company makes it that much more enjoyable. Normally I would have been in better spirits. It was a beautiful night, after all, and the smell of wisteria filled the night air, drifting through my kitchen window, making me dizzy as I continued to feel out of sorts. Every year on approaching my mother's birthday I had the same symptoms. I held the kitchen sink and tilted my head back and shut my eyes and took a slow breath. The night she died, almost twenty years before, she'd left the restaurant early. She'd had a migraine that was making her nauseous, she said, and the smell of food was making it worse. She left before we opened, something she never had done before. I kissed her and told her to go rest, and that I'd check in on her after the first seating, but I forgot. I was busy. And that was the last time I saw her alive.

I was the one who found her the next morning on her couch with one of my father's sweaters lying across her chest. She looked as if she'd just laid down for a little nap, like she'd dozed off, so still and lovely. I later found out that she'd passed away the night before. Tumor, they found out. It had been growing slowly for decades maybe, hidden deep inside her skull. That may have been what was causing her migraines, causing sensitivity to light and mild hallucinations.

I still imagine that she died waiting for the call that I forgot to make. But that night, while preparing dinner for my husband and anticipating his return, I opened my eyes and allowed myself a heavy-hearted sigh. I couldn't help but laugh at the fact that all my dogs had encircled me by the sink. I often told my dogs how much I still missed my mother and they'd thump their tails on the floor, yawn, and stretch, as if getting ready to hear my long-winded story for the millionth time. And that night was one of those nights because the concoction I was making was Yorkshire pudding pie.

Two

Rhubarb red and cinnamon brown-flecked leaves rustled on the timeless maples that lined the neighborhood street I grew up on. Radios played from kitchen windows, scratching and hissing with political jargon and catchy-tuned commercials while teenagers sat in parked cars, snapping their fingers to Elvis and The Beatles. The sidewalks, playfully decorated with rainbow-colored chalk, displayed tic-tac-toe and hopscotch graffiti, while scrappy boys puffed up their young chests over lively games of basketball. Bicycles, like a dumped-out box of colored crayons, lay askew in the middle of driveways and over front lawns that graced quaint houses, each rich in layers of paint and vivid in their own personality.

It was apparent that our street had not been repaved in fifty years, buckled and humped and lined with cracks as it was. It had been filled in places with black tar, as if it were the face of an old wise man that was at the center of it all, watching, observing our lives. It was an older neighborhood even back then, but vibrant young families kept it alive, making memories to be happily recounted years later.

"Without the new," Momo would always say, "the old has no one to tell its story to."

Our house stood alone in its pure white colonial grandeur, along with sweeping baby ivy intent on taking over the entire house. "432" was inlayed into a flat cement block propped up at the foot of our decaying driveway, and alongside it my two tiny handprints, pressed in deep, claimed this address to be our home. This was where I grew up: 432 West Denslow Avenue.

Our community, at any stranger's first glance, was an eccentric place to live. It was a small enclave a few blocks wide and complete with a central village. Westside Village is what it was called, and within its radius we had everything we could ask for. There was a movie theater, a corner coffee shop, and a drug store. A ladies boutique, a fine tailor, a supermarket, a barber, a bank, and a gas station, and one restaurant that changed owners at least once a year until the spring of 1969, but I'll get to that in a bit.

***

My real name is Tutelar, but Momo called me Tutor. Momo was her nickname, too, given to her by my father. Her real name was Monique. Tutelar was the name my father had chosen for their child-to-be, boy or girl, before I was even conceived. Tutelar means "to guard," and that's what my father wanted for my mother, someone to watch over her, particularly if he should not be around to do so himself, given all the traveling he did around the world. My face, along with the rest of me, was little, like a baby doll, with tiny pointed features set deliberately in place. One eye was always hidden behind a sweeping lock of hair, the other exposing their startling blue color with a hint of corn yellow around the iris. By the time I was six years old, my mousy blond hair had a slight tint of mint green, which Momo told me was from too much time in our swimming pool. Playful freckles splashed across my slightly turned up nose, while my lips were constantly stained from watermelon popsicles. I often wore a mischievous grin, and one look at me let you know I had more than a hint of determination.

I was a self-reliant only child and I had a most fantastic imagination. I was never afraid to ask the silliest of questions because, according to my inner voice, everything was always open for question. It helped that my last name was Moot. According to *Miriam-Webster's Dictionary,* moot means, "Open to question or debate, *a moot point*." So, with a name like that, the stage was set for a lifetime full of dreams, answered or not.

On most days after school I would plop upon my stomach on my queen-sized bed, glance around my baby blue and corn yellow bedroom—the color of Raleigh's eyes (and my own)—and try to quickly finish my homework so I could go out and play with my dog. I'd gaze out my bedroom window, watching the other neighborhood girls who were always dressed so pretty with their hair so nice. They were the ones who decorated the sidewalk with big pink flowers or purple monsters with rainbow-colored teeth. They would giggle and laugh and whisper into each other's ears.

I found them odd, or maybe I just couldn't relate to their nonsense and girlish ways. I watched them as they flirted with the neighborhood boys and just shook my head. I had much more important things to do with my time, but their artistry did amuse me. I always imagined that if I liked a boy, I would have told him right to his face. I would have said, *"I think I like you enough—do you want to catch polliwogs with me?"* And that's exactly how I did say it when a new little boy entered my fourth grade class. His name was Scooter Dubrow and he was my very first crush. When my mind started to wander, my thoughts turned to Scooter, who I thought was quite cute, and who caused my heels to click together. All the while I'd chew my pencil like a puppy chomping on a stick. Momo always reminded me not to eat the lead, and that my homework was as important as anything else, and that everything I did in life I should try to do my best. So I did my homework well for myself and for Momo.

My mind was full of questions about other families. Sometimes I would watch the neighborhood hooligans and wonder what they talked about with their families at dinnertime. How many of them actually had something to say to their parents? And were they very interested in whatever their parents had to say?

I wondered how many place settings each house had at dinnertime, and if anyone would say grace or say thank you after a meal. I tried to imagine having a brother or a sister and I couldn't. I thought them all odd, the people who lived on our street, and I never gave a thought as to whether they might have thought the same of us. Momo and I were really the odd ones, I realize now, but only in the very best way. It was just the two of us in that big white house with only two place settings. We didn't say grace, we just shared stories of how our day went and tried to make each other laugh and asked for Raleigh to please come home.

Downstairs in our elegant powder-blue dining room, Momo would set the dinner table for two each evening and seek counsel from the little dogs at her heels on their thoughts on world politics, the weather, or her latest flower arrangement. She would routinely order my dog, the one named HoneyWest, to retrieve me from my room.

"Honey! Tell Tutor dinner is almost ready!" It gave HoneyWest such a feeling of importance, the fury fluff would respond with a grunt and a loud single raspy bark, and in a flash she would take off up the staircase to find her master while the others, Mopsey and Butler, stayed downstairs with one eye always on Momo.

Most afternoons I contemplated the what's and what if's of my small life, pondering my studies and looking out the window to see if anything had changed on the street below. The hooligans would still be there doing the same thing and my accomplice, HoneyWest, always wiggled her way into my bedroom just in time to save me from my boredom. I would giggle at my best friend's attempt at being sneaky, causing her to bark her raspy bark and spin with whiplash speed. This would always cause me to clap my hands in delight and laugh out loud, thus causing Honey to go just a little more crazy with excitement. And during those moments, there was nothing better in the whole wide world: me and my dog sharing the bliss of our complete understanding of each other. Who needed colored chalk anyway?

I would finish my homework to my satisfaction and take one last look at the street below, hoping to maybe see something new, but I never did, and this confirmed for me that my dog was much more entertaining than any hooligan ever could be.

Three

Bon Ton

I was a child of eclectic taste, which was partly my mother's fault for always dressing me up in things the kids at school would laugh at. But for the most part I was, in my mind, modern and ahead of my time, just like Momo.

She had such style, not like the other mothers in their eyelet sundresses and white gloves, flared skirts, and sun hats. No, my mother was a bit of a scene-stealer. Her easy style was earthy yet high fashion, and because of the way clothes hung on her slim figure, it seemed effortless. She always mixed crazy colors and mismatched prints and wore a collection of bracelets, gold and silver, stacked high on her arms, along with funky long chains around her swanlike neck. She seldom wore skirts, always Capri pants cut just above the ankle, and because of her height, flat strappy sandals. A loose blouse or an oversized V-neck sweater of Raleigh's, with the sleeves pushed way up, past all the bracelets, was her standard attire. Her skin was white velvet with only a few faint freckles across her nose and cheeks and chest, and her hair was jet black and glossy, full and wavy with a deep side part that showed off her perfect profile.

Momo was thin but not skinny. She had long graceful fingers and she always wore one big gold ring of brown topaz on her index finger, and, of course, her wedding ring, a single thick gold band, which she hadn't removed since my father placed it there ten years before. My mother was often whispered about when we shopped in the village. Women would pull on their husbands' arms a little tighter when Momo walked by. Everyone who knew her found her to be most engaging, but other women were skeptical of her because of her beauty. She would cheerfully make small talk with the local merchants and always compliment whatever they sold. Eventually, whatever she was wearing that disrupted the neighborhood equilibrium would be copied by a few of the judgmental housewives.

Momo found this flattering yet annoying, and as much as she tried to fit in with the simple mentality that any small town has when it comes to a single woman with a small child, she ultimately dealt with things by keeping to herself, dressing down, and being a gracious neighbor. It would turn out to be the case that she was never recognized for how, whenever she heard of someone in our neighborhood in despair, she would leave a small treat of freshly baked, piping hot Yorkshire pudding with a handwritten card of encouragement on their doorstep. This was not something that was ever done for her after her own despair came knocking seven months before I was born, the night she heard the news that would change everything she had planned.

I, on the other hand, was a little more confusing to my peers. I hated it when I was copied, and made it a point to let everyone know. I went crazy mad for my Go-Go boots. I had them in every color—white, red, orange, blue, even green! No one was as bold as me. My yellow boots, which I was the most mad about, really set me apart. The kids at school made fun and said I peed in my boots whenever I wore them, but I would just tell them they didn't know fashion like I did, that I was "vogue," which is what Momo told me to say.

My boots came in all shapes, some short and pointed, some tall all the way up to my knees. No other little girl had such a collection, so it was, at nine years old, my "thing." The rest of my wardrobe contained items that suited my fancy at the moment— mostly miniskirts and T-shirts, bell bottoms or blue jeans, and my brown leather dress with the big gold zipper up the front, sported with my orange boots, was my ultimate fashion statement. Oh, how I loved that dress and oh, how I was teased for it, but I didn't care. I felt wonderful wearing it.

Momo and I were different in many ways from other families. Being without a husband and a father was something completely out of our control, but there was something else that set us apart that was very much in our control: we were, without a doubt, the very best of friends. Our bonding began before I was born, like most mothers and daughters I imagine, but without tummy rubs and soothing music, long soaks in the tub, or a baby shower. No, ours started out very different indeed.

My mother was out of her mind with fear after two men came to our house in the middle of the night to deliver a fateful message. She was determined not to lose her baby after hearing the devastating news about her husband, my father, Raleigh. She made it her mission to keep me in place for the remaining seven months of her pregnancy. She stayed in bed for the entire week after she heard the news, only getting up to eat a little Yorkshire pudding and to drink a few glasses of milk, until she realized she would crumble to dust without some support. Her parents came to help until she was securely four months pregnant and holding. For the remaining months, Momo talked and walked and planned while I listened, or so she assumed.

She spent afternoons in the park lounging on a blanket eating chocolate-covered pretzels and green sour apples dipped in peanut butter, reading books about how to become a professional dog breeder. It never crossed her mind to read one of Doctor Spock's baby and childcare books. She knew she would be a wonderful mother. The dog breeding idea was her way to keep her thoughts uplifted. By the time I arrived, Mopsey and Butler had already had their first litter of puppies and they considered me one of their own. My father would have been pleased that the little dog he bought to cheer up my mother ended up making such an impact on our lives.

***

My father, Mr. Raleigh William Moot, was tall, sandy-haired, and debonair. He was six-foot-three with long muscular limbs. He was said to be a towhead in his youth, but by the time he met Momo his hair had turned a sandy gray. His skin was golden and weathered and his beard frosted and scruffy. His eyes, Momo said, were his best feature: baby blue with a ring of corn yellow around the iris, just like mine. He was an artist, craftsman, and photographer, and lover of anything that would take him away from the dull humdrum of everyday normal existence. His life was filled with photo shoots, traveling, and deadlines. Raleigh, according to Momo, was always in motion; he was exciting to be around and enthralling to listen to. He had fantastic stories from his many adventures and no one would have ever guessed that he'd come from such humble beginnings. I never knew him in the fatherly sense, so I referred to him as Raleigh in conversation, but he was always my father in my dreams: the dashing man who unwillingly disappeared from my mother's life was a legend to me from the day I was born.

In the early fall of 1958, shortly after Momo and Raleigh moved into the house on West Denslow Avenue but before I was conceived, Raleigh decided to build his future child an old-fashion tree house, nestled in the crook of one of the many oak trees that held court in our whimsical backyard. Inside the organic fort were survival instructions, a flashlight, a canteen, a pocketknife, a compass, a book called *Swiss Family Robinson,* and a leather-bound diary and quill pen, ink included. This way, he thought, if his child was the adventurous yet thoughtful type, he or she would find this a wonderful escape.

When their first baby didn't stick, Momo didn't give up. She coaxed Raleigh to build something else because she knew that the only way he could process his loss was through his creativity. He decided that with any luck his next expectant child just might have a keen business sense, so he worked through his grief, and with renewed hope and my mother's encouragement, he built a grand old-fashion lemonade stand. He named it the "SUM MORE STAND," which he thought was enticing enough. Inside, taped to the side panel, down below, out of sight, were instructions on how to count and make change. When that baby failed to go the distance, he broke down again, and once again my mother encouraged him to build something to relieve his disappointment.

What he created during the third pregnancy turned out to be my fondest memory of childhood. He pined and pondered for weeks, designing and sketching a handmade storybook playhouse, with no instructions necessary. He had thought of everything, except for the fact that the baby might not be a girl. But Momo didn't say a word and made white eyelet curtains for the French windows, and Raleigh carved the name "Tutor" into everything he built: Tutor's Playhouse, Tutor's Tree house, Tutor's "Sum More Stand."

In our backyard, beyond the pool, through the olive trees, rosemary bushes, and purple sage, my playhouse and tree house were built with hopes that I would be born with an active imagination.

As it turned out, all three were a perfect fit for me. They were places where my own small adventures could happen at any time. The playhouse had a white picket fence with fragrant lavender growing all along it, complete with a latched gate to protect the exquisite white cottage that had a red double Dutch door. Within this wonderland was a wishing well, a red swing set, a slide, and a most inviting sandbox filled with the softest pink shimmering sand that Raleigh had brought back, Momo claimed, from a far away magical island.

Momo later added a doghouse and puppy pen, which was always filled with fluffy little black mops, chirping and squeaking, like bumper cars colliding into each other with robust enthusiasm. These smart little rascals also became the most important part of my childhood. They were my crazy little dog siblings, and my comfort when Momo wasn't feeling well, when she had to surrender to the quiet of her bedroom due to her migraines. She still managed to keep a hawk eye on me through a small opening in the drapes. She casually told me years later how cute I was making polite conversation with all the puppies. I smile at the thought to this day.

I arrived fourteen months after the playhouse was finished, but Raleigh wasn't there for my birth or my first birthday or my ninth. Raleigh went missing in an exotic place called Cambodia doing what he enjoyed the most: photography and an adventure. He had, before either one knew that my mother was pregnant for the fourth time, taken an assignment—a special photo assignment for a magazine called *Life*.

Momo and I held out hope for years that Raleigh might have still been alive, that maybe he was being held against his will. It was our dream to hold tight to. Momo was sure he had survived, that it was just a matter of time before he would be back home living happily ever after with us. That is how she managed, what she needed to believe, to numb the loss of Raleigh. My mother was determined to raise me without fear of the unknown, to always be positive and encouraging and kind to others because one never knows who may have gone though something awful in their lives, too.

Years later, Momo talked about how the name of the magazine was ironic, given the assignment ended up taking Raleigh's life. And this is where the Yorkshire terriers made such an impact on us and others with their unconditional love and devotion, their emotional intuition and perception.

Momo said Raleigh named their first Yorkshire Mopsey because she looked like a mop. She was their first baby, Momo would laugh. He gave Mopsey to my mother to keep her company while they were trying to conceive. That was his plan: a soft cute little puppy for Momo to baby until the real baby came along. Mopsey took Momo's mind off a lot of things, including her throbbing temple. The two were inseparable, but as I said before, Momo had an idea—and she started hatching it and me at the same time.

Butler, a two-year-old Yorkie stud, arrived before I was born, shortly after Raleigh's failed return. She bought him to breed with Mopsey and quickly realized what a terrific watchdog he was. Momo thought to breed Mopsey as a way to earn extra money while staying home to raise me. Butler and Mopsey fell madly in love, that's how it all started. I think that was Momo's plan all along: to create a family for us. The fact that they happened to be dogs didn't matter to her: family is family. And in time, the two would sleep every night below my crib, while during the day they'd stand guard, side by side, in front of one of many gopher holes in our yard, waiting. Momo said it was the second greatest love affair of all time.

My mother always had a keen eye about whether or not a puppy was going to a good home, but she insisted that the puppy was the one who decided who to go home with. She was absolutely convinced that there was a divine connection between her puppies and the people she sold them to.

"The Yorkshire terrier," she would say, "is the canine jewel of England, a very devoted breed, sharp as a whip! Snappy, smart, and utterly devoted. So keen is their sense that if given a choice they could even pick who their owners should be."

And that is exactly how Momo conducted her small business from the very start. Of course, in the beginning I was too little to remember all the human-canine connections, but I was aware, by age five, of what was going on.

The puppies came and went as the years went by. The Moot pups were sold to dozens of wonderful families, although sometimes, not very often, someone lonely or broken-hearted would come to buy a puppy and Momo would tear up the check after they left. She'd tell me that the puppy they picked just happened to be the "free" one. I didn't understand then, but she was always in a good mood after a free puppy was bought. And once in a while she would give a puppy away to someone just because her heart told her to. I think it was my mother's destiny to breed those little dogs, to help her cope and forget her own pain and loss, and to bring joy to someone who needed it.

As time ticked on, I started realizing the hope of having a sibling join our small family would never happen since I didn't even have a father, which is why I started making up imaginary fantastic adventures as a way to entertain myself and shut out the absence of Raleigh. Mopsey and Butler and all the puppies kept me distracted from feeling like an only child.

I was grateful for the dogs' affection, and in turn I spent many afternoons after school teaching them tricks like hide and seek, gimme your paw, going down the slide, follow the leader, and go fetch—intensive training I thought at the time. I always rewarded them with a small treat and a scratch behind their ears and a kiss on their wet noses, and the puppies always rewarded me with wagging tails, wanting more of me. They never knew how much I needed them or how they filled up my little soul and taught me what too many humans seem to lack: how to be happy about the little things in life.

Mopsey and Butler were very busy making puppies for the first years of my life. Mopsey had four litters by the time I was seven. As Momo's breeding business flourished, she also built a solid reputation for healthy, smart puppies. Her prices were fair but not cheap, and aside from a few special circumstances, she made good money over those six years. With each new litter, I would thoughtfully name the pups as to their specific personality or looks, and sometimes the new owners would even keep the names for good.

There are a few names I remember to this day. There was Pearl, so perfect and small, with a little white spot on her throat, like a pearl necklace. Hamlet was hardy and hogged all the milk. Midge, the midget, always rubbed her tail end on the carpet. Ninny, so daft yet adorable. Noble, the one in charge, the leader of his litter. And then HoneyWest, the runt of hers. She was blonde like me, odd for a Yorkie, and she had a very hard time when she was born. She came into my life with Mopsey's fourth litter in 1966.

Most litters usually had a runt. According to Momo, they were sometimes the weakest, but somehow always the smartest, and definitely the most determined given just a little help.

HoneyWest didn't say a peep when she entered the world that stressful December night. It was cold outside, not the best time of year for puppies to be born. Momo would always try to plan so the litters would come around late spring so the puppies could enjoy their playpen outside next to my playhouse. That way I could have their company while playing by myself, which was most of the time.

Mopsey had been agitated for days, trying to sneak off to give birth under Momo's bed, so we kept a close eye on her every move. She at last came to Momo and gave her a pleading look that things were about to happen. It went on for hours, a slow process, we thought, because she was just too tired of having puppies. As Mopsey lay exhausted after having delivered five puppies, she didn't have the strength to stimulate the last one who lay limp in the corner. Momo was frantic as she began rubbing the puppy's tiny belly, listening for the faintest squeak or burp of some sort. When nothing seemed to work and HoneyWest lay limp in my mother's hands, Momo began to shake.

Mopsey started to whimper louder and louder as the puppy began to drift away. It was the saddest sound I'd ever heard. Momo quickly thought what to do and ordered me to run fast to the kitchen to get the jar of dark-colored honey, which she always gave me as a remedy when my throat was sore and itchy.

She gently dipped her pinky into the soft amber and held it to the puppy's mouth. Ever so gently, she pushed the honey onto her little pink petal tongue. The puppy started responding, holding Momo's pinky tight with her little mitten-like paws and sucking with all her might. A cough, a burp, and a little wiggle proved to be the cure. With a wink and a smile, Momo handed me my first dog. Within a few days of sucking the sweet amber honey, she grew strong and was just fine, and that's how her name came to be Princess Honey of West Denslow Avenue—HoneyWest for short. It sounded so regal.

Every once in a while a litter comes along and one puppy stands out as extra special, and with that particular litter it was her, my little HoneyWest.

Four

Monique and Raleigh

Momo and Raleigh met in early 1958, just two years before I was born. My mother, a struggling artist with a bohemian spirit, was on vacation with some girlfriends on a hypnotic island with clear blue skies, flower-scented trade winds, and palm trees that bent out toward the purple-blue water.

With not much to do except take in the colors and tranquility, she decided to take a walk along an iridescence sand beach. A tall handsome man approached her claiming to be a photographer for a travel magazine. He started a light conversation about the island's landscape and the ridiculously warm water. Momo had planned this trip to collect her thoughts on life and relationships in general, having just had her heart broken by a conflicted soul who almost convinced her they were destined to be together. At first she was skeptical of Raleigh, but they talked as they walked along the next four picturesque beaches that wrapped around the small island. They philosophized about world events, politics, and the greater good, and by sunset they found that they were right back where they started three hours earlier.

Raleigh asked if she wouldn't mind being his model for a shoot he was doing the next day. She held back her excitement with a slow agreeable nod and explained that she needed to tell her friends, and stipulated that at least one friend needed to accompany them on this so-called photo shoot. He was glad to see she was not too naive, as she was too beautiful, and agreed that having a friend join them would be a good idea.

A moment passed between them when the sun sank behind a huge thundercloud on the ocean's horizon. When the tangerine light pierced through its silver lining, Momo caught her breath and held it, slowly closing her eyes as she made a wish.

Raleigh watched her sunburned face melt to a velvet soft finish, her black hair tangled by the salty beach air and her lips windburned and chapped, curled slightly upward as if she held a great secret. He wished he could capture that image forever, and not just with his camera.

The next day, my mother arrived at the beach without an escort, and Raleigh gave her a slow smile and said, "Let's walk around the island and chase the sun." She nodded and laced her fingers through his.

That moment, finding my mother, was something Raleigh had dreamed of his entire life. He was only a young boy when he needed to find work to support his family. He already had a paper route around his neighborhood, so he asked the manager at the paper for a promotion and quickly worked his way up to assisting running the press. He worked hard, saved his money, and bought his first used camera. He began going out in the field and covering stories and taking pictures on his own and submitting story ideas to the local paper, hoping for a break. He photographed anything the small town would find interesting.

He was from a small fishing village, someplace in North Carolina that was not very exciting. The story goes that his father went fishing one day and never came back, lost at sea the fishermen said, leaving his mother alone with five kids. But Raleigh knew the truth about where his father disappeared to, and her name was Katherine. Raleigh was left to be the man of the house to his mother and four older sisters. His sisters eventually all married, and Raleigh thanked God for that. It was the only way he was finally able to leave and move to Washington DC, where he heard photojournalists could make a good living.

Raleigh remained for some time, however, in the old Craftsman-style house in North Carolina with my grandmother, caring for her for many years, which in itself was unbearable. She was a needy woman and held on to her fear of loneliness and to Raleigh. She never accepted her husband's abandonment and patiently awaited his return until she died in her sleep with the sheets turned down on her husband's side of the bed, his robe and his slippers carefully laid out. My mother told me that days before she died, Raleigh had passed by a store window and seen a large poster ad of a tropical island with a luxury liner in the distance. Raleigh wanted out of his small town and wanted a better job and a better life. He wanted to see the world. As soon as his mother passed, Raleigh sold the house and packed his bags. He already knew where he was going, and unlike his own father, he had no one to leave behind.

***

Momo was raised by two British parents as an only child, just like me, in San Francisco. Early in her youth she yearned to connect with the artistic side of life and embraced anything that unleashed her creative instincts. She learned to bake by her mother's example and to cook with her father in their tiny kitchen.

They owned a European-style restaurant situated in front of their tiny studio apartment, the place where Momo learned the art of the perfect Yorkshire pudding, a family secret. She grew up absorbing the stories her parents told her of the war in Europe and the effects it had on their family. From a young age, Momo worked the restaurant all by herself. She saved all her tips until she graduated from high school, all the while doing well in school and attending youth demonstrations and underground political gatherings. But there was too much tension in the city of San Francisco and she eventually needed a new focus. So she left home with her parents blessings at nineteen. She organized a trip with three girlfriends and they hit the road to see what they could find. What my mother found was not too far from home. Once she discovered Big Sur, she waved goodbye to her friends and they continued their wanderlust without her.

Big Sur was quaint and unpretentiously cultured. It offered an array of opportunities in everything Momo loved: bookstores, art galleries, fine restaurants, funky cafes, a playhouse theater, and eventually love itself. She found her first love one night in a small dingy diner, pondering over a tattered letter, dragging hard on a cigarette and hovering over a cup of coffee.

My mother was transfixed by how tragically exquisite he was and wondered what kind of woman must have written that tattered letter he caressed so dearly, for it could only have been a broken heart that reduced a man like him to such deep reflection on a rainy night in a depressing diner. *A vision out of a romance novel,* she thought, and unbeknownst to her she was about to be cast as the leading lady.

My mother and James ended up being happy for a while. They were twenty in the late 1950s, on the cusp of a new movement, a new decade, a new time. There was an up-and-coming Senator who was young and handsome and hopeful. The youth of America embraced him. It was all so exhilarating.

Momo worked hard to support them both, waiting tables at night and managing an art gallery during the day, while James strained to be politically motivated and lazy at the same time. Holding a job was not one of his strong suits. As it turned out, James came from a strict military background and detested anyone who tried to put him in his place. He was righteous and angry and he embraced a negative attitude of America for its involvement in things that were none of America's business. He strived to emulate a young truth-seeker by the name of Kerouac, whom he was nothing like. He wanted to live like the Beatniks and kiss off the establishment. He went against the grain of patriotism and anything involving the military. His obsession with the threat of war only made his attitude worse, and fanned the flames of battle he had in his heart against his father, a Sergeant Major in the Army. Momo was not someone who gave up on anything very easily and just kept hoping he would change. She was torn: she loved his depth and passion, but he was trying too hard to be something he was not: a free spirit.

Momo unexpectedly found James's future one day at the restaurant while waiting on a woman who was clearly not a local. She was dressed in finely tailored clothes and coat with a fur-trimmed collar and cuffs. When Momo approached her to take her order she was staring blankly out the window, holding her shoulders and head high.

My mother gently topped off the woman's cold coffee and noticed the magazine beside her cup of coffee. The cover photograph was disturbing and clearly was supposed to be. My mother, transfixed by the image, thought to herself how fortunate she was to live in America. The image was of a screaming woman, clothes torn, slash marks across her neck, chest, and face, clutching a nude limp baby and standing waist-high in a swampy river, as a soldier in the distance pointed a gun toward her.

The woman cleared her throat as to dismiss my mother from the table and at that moment the resemblance and attitude was clear. It was James's mother—she was sure of it. As it turned out, she had come to Big Sur to bring her only son home, back to his respectable position in the family, to fulfill his father's expectations of carrying on his military achievements. James's father was a proud and stubborn man who, as a high-ranking official, was ashamed that his only son had not an ounce of honor, having chosen the life of a rebellious ingrate. James would not, could not, lead any other type of life other than the one that was laid out for him, if his father had any say in the matter. The Sergeant Major sent James's mother to bring him to his senses and to bring him home. When my mother went to their apartment that night after her shift she found it void of any trace of James except for the letter she'd seen him reading the night she first laid eyes on him. She said he'd left it to explain his leaving. All that time she assumed it was from a woman he must had loved, and she was right; it was from James's mother telling him his father was ill and she needed him to come home.

The photographer of that tragic image on the magazine cover went on to win the Nobel Prize. He was unknown until that photograph was taken, and unbeknownst to my mother, he, not James, would be the person to change her life forever.

***

After his mother died in 1956, Raleigh's life took flight. He simply faked his way to unexpected success. He had an extremely artistic eye for photography, some not-so-bad writing skills, and the desire to see the world. Plus, he had no one to answer to. To his satisfaction, this opened up a lot of traveling opportunities. He had established himself as a go-getter and was offered a chance to do some research in what he was told was a small, slightly inflamed situation in a place called Vietnam. The U.S. wasn't involved militarily, but interest was building given its communistic attitude. He would be going on media assignment for the purpose of taking notes and a photo or two. He wouldn't be gone for more than just a few months, they told him. He thought it was a good opportunity and that he would take some action photos and try to sell them when he returned to make some extra money. He ended up, after a lot of coaxing from fellow photographers in DC, submitting the photos to a famous magazine called *Life* that published my father's photos, one of which landed the cover and went on to win my father the esteemed Pulitzer Prize, as well as a job with *Life* as a staff photographer.

Having been recognized for his vision, Raleigh was very sought after, and it kept him extremely busy. But he had decided something while he was away, too: that he had seen enough horrific things to last him a lifetime and he wanted nothing more to do with that. He wanted to see the beauty in the world and to capture "that" with his camera.

He claimed a simple life, and humbly and happily worked for a travel and leisure magazine. It wasn't very ambitious, but after what he'd seen—the conflict and its atrocities which made him weep at random moments and realize how he wanted to live his life—he vowed to only photograph "pretty people" doing "lovely things" in "beautiful places." *Social Status* magazine is where he went to work, and it soon became a worldwide staple for socialites and the rich and famous, and just like that he created a new career for himself.

When my parents met that splendid day on the beach someplace in the South Pacific, their destiny was already in motion, but they could never have imagined how brief their encounter would be.

Five

The first week on the island my parents met every day for a cup of coffee and a walk on the beach; the second week, they met every day for a picnic lunch on the beach; by the third week, it was dinner by candle light every night on the hotel terrace as they watched the moon's reflection break into a million cuts of light onto the pounding surf.

When the end of the month arrived too soon and it was time for them to go their separate ways, they shared breakfast together. Raleigh carried my mother's in to her on a tray with a small vase that held a single gardenia flower. Kismet is how they met, she would always tell me as she recalled how oddly and sweetly suited to one another they were. She felt everything between them seemed to happen for a reason and was perfectly fine with Raleigh's erratic work schedule. He always had to travel to more beautiful places to snapshot more interesting people doing more exotic things, but now he brought Momo along as his personal model and assistant. He would have it no other way.

He thought her to be the perfect accent to whatever scenery or hotel, landmark or fountain, Villa or yacht that the magazine might want to feature in its next issue. She was his muse, and the backdrop to everything that mattered to him. Their love affair was tangible yet capricious, full of spontaneity and excitement. Until the day my mother screamed on an Aspen mountaintop while modeling a white fur coat high up on a chair lift. Raleigh and his crew thought it was the altitude, since it had, after all, caused her to feel faint earlier that day, but in fact it was a stabbing pain in her belly that made her yell out that day.

She was pregnant, not far along, and it would turn out to be the first of several miscarriages. My parents cried in each other's arms that afternoon in the warmth of their cabin. Tender flakes of snow shimmered in the late afternoon light as they fell into a deep sleep until dawn. Raleigh smiled into my mother's eyes the next morning as a judge, the photo crew, and the fur shop owner witnessed their union of love at a small Aspen church on a vividly beautiful day.

After the photo shoot wrapped up, they headed west to California. It was the fall of 1958 and they settled into town and bought what would be their first and only home at 432 West Denslow Avenue.

My mother loved the neighborhood and the little village that came with it. It was old-fashioned and timeless, as everyone knew everybody's business, good or bad, and one could never feel lonely living on West Denslow, or walking around the village, and this turned out to be a good thing in the years to come for Momo and me.

Raleigh traveled less frequently, taking odd photography jobs closer to home with not such luxurious accommodations so he could be home in no time if Momo needed him. They had no trouble at all making babies together, but a hard time making them stick. Everything else for them was almost too perfect. Having a child was not.

A few anticipated announcements were put on hold one too many times and finally my mother was advised by her doctor to stop the obsession with having a baby—that she just could not, would not, ever carry a baby to full-term. Again they cried in each other's arms and for weeks they could barely look each other in the eyes, each blaming themselves for their misfortune.

After four miscarriages, my parents found themselves at home in the kitchen sitting in silence. It was spring of 1959 and Raleigh, as always, was watching my mother cook while he sipped a short glass of whiskey and glanced over a pile of negatives. She was making his favorite dish of braised beef with turnips and sweet figs, but she was also attempting to try something different. She normally made soda biscuits to soak up the sweetness of the wine and figs, but she'd been missing her parents, especially as she was struggling so with not being able to have a baby of her own, and she decided to make something that reminded her of them. They had moved back to England not too long after she'd left San Francisco for Big Sur. So she'd settled on making Yorkshire pudding that night, a recipe that always reminded her of home, and of her parents, and which she hadn't made in years.

In England, in her parents' hometown, she explained to Raleigh, they had a Sunday tradition of roast beef and Yorkshire pudding. The puddings were like small soufflé pockets, a pancake batter sort of mixture that was baked and then drenched or dipped in the roast beef juices. It was a cheap and filling way to feed a large family during hard times or war, since meat was expensive.

She was caught up in her thoughts and kept on rambling, and my father thought her irresistible. "Another recipe," she went on excitedly, "was to bake a sausage right into the middle of the batter, which they called a toad in the hole! So maybe one day I might make a pie of all this—a Yorkshire pudding pie." She laughed in her lyrical way and returned to her project with a crooked smile. Raleigh felt a moment of relief as her enthusiasm for this tradition seemed to lift her sprits, if only for a moment. She stayed up all night perfecting the pudding, making sure it was just right, because nothing else in her life seemed to feel that way.

What would be my crib stood empty in the nursery, cold and sterile, untouched. Momo, isolated with her thoughts and her nesting that had no hope for an outlet, began to compulsively bake Yorkshire pudding. She gave the warm fluffy pockets to anyone she thought needed a little comfort. She would wrap them up, piping hot, in brown paper bags tied with a simple string. Nothing fancy.

Although the Yorkshire pudding was well received by all our neighbors, including the mailman, the pool man, and the gardener, Momo kept adjusting her recipe. Her headaches were visiting more often during this creative time and her determination was unyielding. Raleigh felt so strained as he watched her day after day try to extinguish her misery through her constant baking of the Yorkshire pudding that he decided to do something about it.

A few weeks prior he'd had a photo shoot at a famous actress's home in the countryside of Northern England. She was divine, refined, and very British. She posed elegantly in every room of her beautiful, sprawling English Tudor estate. As the shoot came to an end, she demurely asked to be photographed with her six-year-old pride and joy. Raleigh, of course, was thrilled to extend the shoot to the stables, where the thoroughbreds were doted upon. He envisioned finishing the shoot with a prized champion stud. She excused herself graciously and in a matter of minutes returned with her pride and joy: a four-pound, flaxen-maned "troll," as Raleigh laughed to recall, was draped over her forearm, crowned with a fountain of flowing silver hair held up in a tight rhinestone-studded clip.

"Raleigh, meet Prim," the elegant woman said.

Raleigh's photo of the actress and her little dog named Prim sitting in her lap landed the cover of *Social Status,* and overnight the popularity of the Yorkshire terrier and the magazine skyrocketed.

Within days of its publication, Raleigh made a call to the actress telling her of his affection for Prim and how he wanted to find a little female just like her for his wife. The actress, thrilled to be of help to her now favorite photographer, sent him the contact information for the breeder, who lived in Yorkshire, England. The purchased puppy was shipped first-class on the lap of a pretty stewardess the following week, arriving just in time for Easter.

***

The evening the dog arrived was a moment my mother said she would never forget. She was in the kitchen baking more Yorkshire pudding, exhausted and frustrated, her temples throbbing with pain, when my father came home. He stopped short of the kitchen entry and called her name: "Monique"— something he only called her in serious moments. She turned slowly, wiping the flour from her hands and off her forehead and gave my father a sad smile, thinking what a thoughtful husband he was. He toted in one arm a bucket of Kentucky Fried Chicken and a bottle of Dom Pérignon, and the other he held behind his back.

Momo melted seeing his smile, the way his ears turned bright red when he held a secret. He leaned back and placed whatever he was holding behind his back onto the floor. It was unclear to Momo what it was at first, but then the yapping black ball of fur charged straight toward her. She bent down and picked it up in one swoop, and fell madly in love with the most adorable puppy she had ever seen.

Raleigh had already named her Mopsey because she so resembled a mop. His eyes beamed, she said, and my soulful mother, with grateful tear-filled eyes, stared straight into Raleigh's eyes for the first time in months. My father's intuition was right: Momo and Mopsey were inseparable. She took her new puppy everywhere she went. She fixed her mane into a spiky ponytail on top of her head and tied it with a bow. She could be seen toting the little mop in a red leather shoulder bag around town. The added surprise was Mopsey's pedigree—that the Yorkshire terrier truly was from England made her all the more special in Momo's heart. Mopsey, meanwhile, filled her position beautifully, with personality and unconditional love and devotion. My mother didn't take a breath without the alert attention of her new sidekick.

Mopsey would most likely have kept her distracted forever, pushing my mother's baby thoughts down deep, but just as everything else in my mother's life seemed to go in a cosmic direction, so did I.

I entered the picture that same night Raleigh gave Mopsey to my mother. I was created that evening, unbeknownst to them, in the spirit of Easter and rebirth. A toast of champagne, a feast of fried chicken, a sleeping puppy in a basket at the foot of the bed, and my parents wrapped in each other's arms made me come true. Momo said it was the most romantic night of her life, a moment that still sweeps through her chest and makes her catch her breath.

The next morning, the sudden alarm of the phone woke them. Raleigh received word that *Life* wanted him back for one special assignment, back to the place he knew as hell on earth. He failed to tell my mother that day, or even in the weeks that followed. He worried that it would destroy their rekindled romance, because Raleigh had in fact requested the assignment. Though he was happy working with *Social Status* magazine, in the sad months with Momo he'd begun to feel the itch for adventure.

My parents spent those next few weeks very much in love, happy at last with just their little dog and their cozy home. As their time together was coming to an end, they were also unaware that I had been conceived, or that one short month was the only time the three of us would all be together—ever. Momo's mood had shifted after Mopsey's arrival and Raleigh was relieved. She'd at last found the exact ingredients to perfect her Yorkshire pudding, not realizing I was now along for the ride, though I most likely had inspired her taste buds, if only just a bit.

Life felt warmer with Mopsey around to lift her sprits, she told Raleigh over and over as she held her puppy. She cried softly when he finally told her he would be going away for a short while. He'd put it off as long as he could, as he feared her reaction, but she told him she was a big girl and would be just fine, not to worry about her while he was overseas and that all she wanted was for him to be happy—that if going on assignment was what he needed for a little adventure then she thought it was important. She would support his decision. She smiled and squeezed her little dog and said, "I wont be alone. I have Mopsey now." She said just to hold Mopsey and pet her human-like hair and have those sweet black eyes watching her every move made her feel less lonely. Somehow the little dog soothed the dull pain she had learned to live with and hide from everyone. It worked even after Raleigh left, at least until the evening a priest and young military officer came knocking at the break of dawn three months after Raleigh flew east. Thank God she'd been able to send word to him about the pregnancy, letting him know that the baby would be just fine.

Everything was planned, that's what she kept telling herself. They were supposed to pick up right where they'd left off as soon as he returned. She had decorated the nursery a few times over, but she needed Raleigh's opinion. He was the one with the fine eye for beauty. She painted the room corn yellow; she thought he'd like that, to suit a girl or a boy, and hung stars and a moon over the crib. A rocking chair that he had made for her just before he left sat by the window that overlooked the street below, where she could watch the children play while she rocked their baby, he had told her.

He had built the tree house and the playhouse, and the confection stand during those months when they kept trying and failing to have a baby. Each of them came with handwritten instructions for how to enjoy these things he'd created. My mother knew that he wanted the baby be named Tutelar, whether it was a boy or girl, and he'd engraved the name on the tree house, the playhouse, and the Sum More Stand.

Momo had at last perfected her Yorkshire pudding and was very pleased with herself—and she had a terrific idea for a small business. She was just waiting to tell Raleigh about it in person. She was also finally free of her awful migraines, and her doctor said that maybe the pregnancy was balancing out her hormones, that maybe it always was just an imbalance. She was excited to tell Raleigh this news, too, because she knew how much he worried, how much he loved her, how much he missed her.

But instead Momo was told that he and his photography crew had been sent to a place where communication was difficult. The jungle was engulfing, and they may have been disoriented and lost, or they may have been captured. They weren't sure of anything other than the fact that they hadn't heard from the crew in days. So she waited and sat in that rocking chair each evening and stared out the window and slowly rocked and held her hand on her growing belly while her little dog Mopsey kept a vigil eye on both her and the door: they were both waiting for Raleigh to find his way back home.

***

Raleigh did find out about me, about my mother being pregnant. My mother, who had been waiting until she was safely into her second trimester, sent a telegram to the army base, where they claimed to have hand-delivered the news to him just before his fateful excursion. It was said that Raleigh jumped in the air and clicked his heels, pulled out a canister, and offered a swig of whiskey to his crew. Then he toasted loudly, "To Tutelar! My child-to-be!"

That part of the story that got relayed back to her gave Momo comfort, because the description of how it played out let her know that Raleigh, without a doubt, had gotten the news. He had taken out an insurance policy just in case, with a substantial amount of money, enough to provide my mother with a comfortable life without the worry of having to take on a job, at least for a while. It was only a precaution, since he'd intended on getting home. After all, they had a baby to raise together. And he hoped it would be a girl.

Six

Mrs. Van Steenkiste, Spring 1969

HoneyWest and I were inseparable, it was just that simple. From the very start, she followed me everywhere. If she got distracted by something and I kept on walking, she would bark in frustration for me to wait for her. She slept curled beside my neck, I think so she could hear my breath while we dreamt. Where I stood, there she was—at my feet with one paw on my toes, and she always had at least one eye on me, just like my mother.

She was my "third wheel," Momo would say, and she and I often sat on the back stoop together enjoying a Popsicle as we watched the clouds drift by. Ours was the perfect friendship, and I was grateful to have her, especially because I had to let go of our other puppies as they got sold off to other families, never to be seen again.

My mother's business turned into a revolving door of people coming in and puppies going out. I never got used to it, but I was also never disappointed in the new owners—until Mrs. Van Steenkiste, that is. Momo assured me she would never sell a puppy to someone who failed The Test, and The Test of course had to do with Momo's intuition about who would best suit the puppies' personalities. "It's up to the pup, Tutor," she would assure me, and Momo was never ever wrong. But a few times I did have my doubts.

Mrs. Vivian Van Steenkiste had been a widow for fifty years. She and her husband, Porter, had one child, a daughter who was just one year old when he passed away from a horrible illness called meningitis that was so awful it turned his hair white overnight, or so they say. The story is that he had clung to life—and his love for Vivian—for a week in intensive care; in isolation for fear the virus may be contagious. Vivian would scale the fire escape every day to peek through his hospital room window just to make sure he knew she was waiting for him to recover.

Porter was a guarded man—of his feelings and of Vivian. He was the silent type and his formidable size made him quite intimidating. Out in public, he held Vivian close, always escorting her with a gentle hold of her elbow. Men didn't stare for too long to admire his delicate wife because of her great beauty; they stared because of how they appeared together. She was the lamb and he was the lion, or so it looked. In truth, however, Porter was just madly in love with his wife. She made him laugh with her sarcasm and beam with her confidence and only Porter knew, in the privacy of their home, that Vivian was a force to be reckoned with, as she was the lioness and he the lamb.

On his eighth day at the hospital, while Vivian stood on the fire escape with balloons in her hand and their daughter on her hip, he left them with a smile and one single tear that welled up in the corner of his eye.

Vivian and Porter had a love so strong that everyone was sure Vivian would not endure the loss of him. But she did because he told her to enjoy her life, to care for their child, and because she believed that one day they would be together again. She moved forward and raised her daughter on her own with a quiet heart and she marched through life with a set jaw, never letting love in or out. The only tenderness she ever displayed was the gentle touch she gave a silver-framed wedding photo each night before she went to sleep. This was her only consolation; it ensured a peaceful sleep and a stroll down memory lane with her beloved husband, and the tear she held in the corner of her own eye never ever went away.

In the early spring of 1969, Mopsey's new litter was ready for their new homes. A parade of potential owners came and left with and without puppies. Momo was always cautious, scrutinizing every motive someone might have for wanting a puppy. So Mrs. Van Steenkiste hardly seemed like a contender from the very start. When she arrived and curtly informed Momo that she would be picking out a dog for her daughter and three grandsons, I felt sick. She wore a chocolate brown tweed suit that tightly fit her petite frame. She wore a dusty pink silk scarf draped around her neck and swept up to her collarbone, clapped with a large diamond broach that looked like a peacock. Her leather gloves, also a pale pink, were held firmly in her hand, and her brown crocodile clutch, to match her crocodile pumps, was tucked safely between her arm and ribcage. Her silver-blue hair and make-up were immaculate, as was her precision manicure. She was serious and petulant and I couldn't stand her. My mother tried to convince her that maybe a shepherd or a nice mutt would be a better match for three young boys, but Mrs. Van Steenkiste turned up her nose and pointed, "That one!" And with that she scooped up Noble. The puppy gazed up at Mrs. Van Steenkiste, stared at her for the longest time and sniffed into her scarf, taking in her sweet perfume. Mrs. Van Steenkiste seemed flustered and annoyed with the puppy's instant affection and handed him abruptly back to me. "He will have to do. I don't have the time or patience to dog shop. Will you take a personal check?" She wrote in the amount of $500.00 with a trembling hand.

Momo agreed with a smile and a nod and suggested that the puppy could be returned if things didn't work out. I was very disturbed at this decision and retreated to the back stoop with HoneyWest. "It was not a good match!" I told her, though HoneyWest refused to look at me. I said I thought the woman was "nasty" and that her grandsons were probably "nasty" too.

"Tutor!" Momo yelled out. "Never judge someone you know nothing about!" She stood at the back door and sighed before smoothing the front of her slacks and leaving. I know now that she spoke from experience, having been judged over the years by some of the locals. But I held tight to my suspicion about Mrs. Van Steenkiste.

She came back with an assuring smile, as well as a watermelon Popsicle for me. As always, Momo's warm smile was followed by a wink and a nod, to which HoneyWest would grunt and snort. They had some sort of secret code between them and it annoyed me to no end. HoneyWest mustered up a few barks to cheer me up, and I wrapped my arms around my mother and looked up at her as she looked up to the sky with a lovely smile on her face. My unease dissipated and I went off to my playhouse, making my rounds on the swing, the slide, and the sandbox before finally ending up at the cottage to rest and enjoy an imaginary cup of sweet hot tea with

HoneyWest, Mopsey, and Butler, who always stood guard at the door.

Time ticked on and summer was around the corner. Those cold back-to-school days were long gone and the sun sparkled brighter as spring started showing its pretty face. I did my homework as best I could, gazed out my bedroom window like I always would, and watched the neighborhood girls flirt as they colored the sidewalk with monsters and flowers while the boys teased and sparred, popping wheelies down the street.

I still thought them odd. I would retreat to my playhouse and read to HoneyWest while Momo made her Yorkshire pudding and braised beef. It was her favorite recipe, and she often reminisced about Raleigh when she made it. The intoxicating aroma would sweep into my playhouse and through the whole neighborhood with its sweet allure. Rosemary and fig, lavender and thyme, and a hint of sweet ginger. When I think back now and close my eyes, I conjure up the smell and realize that she must have continued to cook that meal to make her feel closer to Raleigh. She didn't talk about him much, sometimes here and there but only with a sigh or to say that one day he might come home, and that we'd just have to wait and see. So she'd braise her beef and make her Yorkshire pudding. She was hoping, I know now, that its sweet aroma would help Raleigh find his way home.

It was how my mother maintained a connection to him; it's how I felt in my playhouse—as if he were sitting on one of the miniature chairs enjoying a cup of tea with me and describing his latest travels. Everything he'd made was a symbol to me that he was thinking of me when he created it, and it made me feel like I knew him.

***

The shifting of the seasons, when the big hand on our clock is pushed forward and the sky seems to tilt up to the heavens with wispy flat streaks of hot pink and gold, casting warm shadows off of the trees, reminds me of the time my mother, without saying a word, showed me that connections can indeed be made with people who are no longer with us. And that it can happen to just about anyone at anytime.

The spring of 1969 was when I first realized there was something special about our dogs. Momo had been aware of the connections being made between our dogs and their owners for a long time. She said it started long before, when I was just a baby. She said it happened with the very first litter Mopsey ever had. Witnessing what was occurring firsthand helped her let go of her sadness and longing for Raleigh. She was then able to replace that sadness with acceptance and maybe a little faith, knowing that people, and even animals, come into our lives to teach and show us things, however small those things may be. That everything really does happen for a reason.

I was in my playhouse describing to HoneyWest what was by now a full-blown crush on Scooter when Momo knocked gently on the door. She entered quietly with that assuring smile and a letter in her hand. She pushed up the sleeves of her sweater, causing her bracelets to jingle lightly. Then she pushed her hair behind one ear and sat next to me on the floor. She smelled so sweet, like figs and flowers, and she scooted close as if to whisper.

"Tutor, Sweetheart, this letter is addressed to you," she said as she looked at me with a bit of caution in her eyes. I'd never received a letter before and I couldn't imagine who would possibly want to write to me. Momo sensed my apprehension and slowly opened the letter and started to read.

Dear Miss Moot,

I send you this letter with embarrassment. It did not seem such a wise choice giving the puppy to my daughter and grandsons after all. You see, the puppy never made it to my daughter's house . . .

Shocked and angered, I glared at my mother and began to cry. My skin prickled and my freckled face contorted as I covered my burning red ears and began to sob. HoneyWest approached me and pawed my leg. Momo gently pulled down one of my hands and continued to read.

The puppy, I soon realized, took a liking to me. This Noble puppy has decided on me. I say this with much elation, as he now resides at my home.

My eyes blinked back the tears and my heart raced. "Go on!" I cried. Momo tried to not show emotion or smile, I think to show me a serious lesson, and then pressed on.

I have kept his name, Noble, as my late husband, Porter, was a very noble man who I much admired and miss deeply.
Together Noble and I go for long walks and relaxing drives to the beach. He is a social fellow and very much the gentleman. He says hello to everyone with his sweet eyes, and he walks with such dignity, with his tail high up and always right on my heel. He sits on my lap on the park bench while I throw crumbs to the pigeons. We watch television together on the couch and dine together every evening at the kitchen table. Noble has his own chair, of course.
He helps me in the garden with his keen sniffer, always pointing out any new menacing gopher holes I may have missed, and when we visit my grandsons, they are always very respectful of him. At the end of our day he sleeps well, for his position is at the foot of my bed, wrapped in my fur stole, protecting me in the still of the night. My heartache has melted away. He is, to my amazement, my very best friend, and he oddly reminds me of my late husband, Porter. Thank you for realizing this for me; my stubbornness is my worst enemy.

Sincerely,
Vivian and Noble Van Steenkiste

I sat stunned, salty chalk streaks streaming down my cheeks, which were now flushed with embarrassment. Momo gave me wink and a nod. "I always pick the right person for our puppies, Sweetheart. Dinner in fifteen minutes." And with that she kissed me on the forehead and then the tip of my nose, licked her thumb, and wiped at my salty cheeks—something I'd always hated until that moment. She gave a gentle stroke to HoneyWest before quietly leaving the cottage.

She gave a heavyhearted sigh as she softly shut the door halfway. From the window, I watched her walk to my swing set and stop. I wondered if she was all right, and then smiled to myself as she sat on the swing and started swinging as high as she could, trying to catch a glimpse over the treetops, I guessed. She was just fine; my beautiful mother was just fine. She smiled with her eyes shut tight. Soon I joined her on the other swing and together we held hands and pumped back and forth, wind in our hair and the cool crisp afternoon breeze on our cheeks. She didn't open her eyes and we didn't talk; we just ebbed and flowed until the trees were a silhouette against the ocean-blue sky. I think she was thinking of Raleigh. I know I was thinking of him, of how it could have been, just the three of us, and it felt just perfect.

Seven

Scooter Pie

I remember feeling my heart flutter. I had never felt shy in front of anyone before. I thought boys were inferior, but Scooter got my attention from the moment I saw him. Our teacher introduced the new boy who was forced to stand in the front of the class as Steven Dubrow, also known as Scooter. I immediately recognized him, as he lived in my neighborhood. I'd often seen him playing basketball with his older brothers in their driveway down the street from my house.

When the family had first moved in the previous summer, I was relieved to hear from the neighborhood gossip girls that Scooter would be attending a private school, which put my mind at ease. They'd moved to California from Texas—Scooter and his five teenage brothers and sisters and their parents. He got a poor start at the private boys school, it seemed, so he transferred to our modest public school just a few months before the school year was coming to the end. This took me by surprise, and it was the last thing I needed. He'd already distracted me enough, and now I was going to see him every day until summer rolled around.

He stood perfectly still, one hand in his back pocket the other in his front, one foot slightly turned and sporting an unlaced dirty blue tennis shoe. I felt an impulse to tie his laces. He wore jeans and a red hooded zip-up sweatshirt with a white T-shirt. His hair was light brown, longer than the other boys', with chunks of blond that contrasted his very dark full eyebrows. His face was sunburned and his nose was slightly peeling on the tip, and his eyes . . . I couldn't look at them directly.

I was disturbed. My mind raced and I had butterflies in my stomach once again. He sat in front of me, two rows up, so I could only see the back of his head, which was fine with me because if he looked my way I would have looked away.

I went home that day, on his first day at my school, on the same bus as Scooter Dubrow, grateful that he again sat in front of me so he couldn't see the dumb smile on my face. I usually told Momo everything that went on at my school, but Scooter was my secret. She asked me if I was getting along with the other kids because I stopped wearing my snappy outfits, and stopped letting my hair hang loose.

As the days and weeks passed, the other little girls at my school went crazy for Scooter's attention. I did not. I sat behind him every day and never looked him in the eye when I passed his desk. In the beginning, he looked at me strangely when I wore my Go-Go boots, but I fixed that quickly by shoving them to the back of the closet and downplaying my curious style. I asked Momo to pull my hair back tight into a ponytail without a ribbon. The girls turned on each other, fighting in the lunch and coat lines, taking cuts to be next to Scooter Dubrow. I did not. I always went to the end of the line so I could keep my eye on him without him knowing.

***

I went about the end of the school year same as usual except that I found myself straining to locate Scooter on the playground. Weeks passed and his popularity only grew. His parents had bought the oldest and largest house on our street. It had the biggest swimming pool I had ever seen, with a diving board that his brothers did front and back flips off of every weekend at their family barbeques. Even in the pouring rain, his family liked to swim. I thought it was because they were from Texas.

Scooter's mother was very nice, and over time she became one of the few friends Momo had. Momo said Mrs. Dubrow was Miss Texas before she was Mrs. Dubrow, though I never understood exactly what she meant by that. Her hair was big and very blond and her white teeth always had a little red lipstick smeared on them. My mother told me that the reason Scooter was so much younger than his brothers and sisters was because his father went away to fight in the war when Scooter's siblings were little. When Mr. Dubrow returned, he and Mrs. Dubrow made Scooter together. "To show Mrs. Dubrow just how much he missed her," Momo told me. I laugh now; it was my mother's first attempt at sex education. I was confused, but I let her think I understood. Momo always told it to me straight.

By April, Scooter had noticed me, and he wasn't very friendly about it either. He deliberately went behind me in line and tugged on my ponytail, only enough to make me look like a fool when I yelled at him to "Stop it!" He made fun of my name and my lunch box that I was very fond of—Barbie, of course. He challenged me on the playground to handball, tetherball, and four square, always reducing me to shame, but not tears. Little girls cried, but not me. If he saw me around the neighborhood, he ignored me but continued to poke fun at me in school, until at last I had enough. I announced on the bus ride home one day that I had a bunch of new puppies at my house and asked if anyone would like to see them. It was Mopsey's newest litter. Then I had his attention; I was now in the driver's seat.

Scooter snapped his head at my announcement and followed me home that day, along with a few others. I held court as I showed my classmates how to handle the puppies. Mopsey was trusting and happy to have visitors admiring her offspring. The pups were tiny and black and made everyone gasp at how cute they were. Momo watched from a distance, proud of her daughter's expert instruction on how to handle a puppy. And Scooter, after that, had a different idea of me. We became friends, but he still picked on me, and I was happy about that because Momo said it meant he really liked me a lot.

Eight

Mr. Early

April leapt into May, and the annoying crows that chimed their annoying "caw caws" were back, and with even more determination it seemed. And they were intent on invading the only neglected house on our street. My classmates and, I toting our books and lunch pails, marched to and from the bus stop each day. We pounded on our lunch pails to shoo away the crows who claimed the dilapidated old house. It was an act of kindness, really, for we all knew that inside its peeling shutters and ramshackle roof lived a man in despair.

As long as I could remember the old man who lived next door was an enigma. He lived alone and never had any visitors. His house, once a proud beautiful beacon of the neighborhood, now creaked and hissed from decay—ever since the passing of his beloved. Before I was born, he and his wife would sit together on warm summer evenings on the house's elegant porch swing, imagining how their unborn children would someday frolic on the front yard, slaying dragons and building forts in the old oak trees.

In the years since his wife had passed, Momo occasionally knocked on Mr. Early's door that he never answered and left a gift of warm Yorkshire pudding, laced with fresh rosemary to lift the old man's sprits. He responded by returning the brown paper bag with the string rolled up inside to our doorstep, seemingly in the middle of the night. To Momo, it was the best "thank you" in the world.

She thought of giving this unhappy man a puppy, knowing that it would surely give some comfort to his loneliness, she would say. I knew to not say a word. I would tell HoneyWest my thoughts, as it weighed heavy on my heart. I was troubled by my mother's benevolence. The thought of one of our puppies having to live in that house with that old man disturbed me to no end.

"His name is Albert, and he was once married to a lovely woman named Elda," Momo told me, trying to bring some compassion into my steeled heart. "He met her while stationed in Hawaii, and together they survived the terrible attack on Pearl Harbor, which happened on a beautiful December Sunday in 1941.

My mother had tried to explain to me as best she could that there had been a great war on the other side of the world years before; it was where Scooter's father had gone to fight. After that, Albert had to leave Hawaii and Elda to fight the Japanese. Albert survived that, too, and came home to marry Elda. They built the house of their dreams, and started their plans of having a family together. They inspired everyone around them with their romantic love and total devotion. When their nest was at last ready, a few years into their marriage, they anticipated that children would soon fill the rooms. They would play and slay dragons on its front lawn, build forts in its trees, and, while the children were fast asleep, Albert and Elda would rock on their porch swing and talk about their day. It was a lovely dream.

Their future, however, took an unexpected turn when Albert's nightmares from the war began to haunt him.

Years had passed since the war, so no one, including the VA psychiatrist, could account for why the ghastly images he reported crept into his dreams so many years into a happy normal life. But nonetheless, they arrived with a vengeance and they tore Albert and Elda's dream of having a family apart. Albert was remorseful beyond words when his terrors lashed out and struck Elda, more than once, in the still of the night. His volatile thrashing, and his babbling in a language so foreign it was impossible to decipher, made it even more frightening.

Over time his terrors escalated to the point where he several times almost killed his wife. Elda, a strong earthy woman, withstood an enormous amount — a black eye and a broken nose — but she always remained sympathetic to the fact that Albert was completely unaware of what he was doing. She took to sleeping in the guest room, and the nightmares seemed to have passed until one night when she saw him sleepwalking through the house in the middle of the night with a knife in his hand.

Elda, a religious woman, was convinced that the devil himself had taken over Albert's soul, and moved out that very night while her sleeping husband tossed and kicked, crying out, lost in a nightmare of some place too distant to grasp. Scared and shaken for the last time, she could stand no more and left their beautiful home to waste away, along with Albert, alone with his demons and endless nightmares.

***

The sun rose and set for years and Albert intently waited for Elda to return. At first, he waited on the porch swing, and then, over time, he would just occasionally peer through the curtains, hoping to see a taxi pull into the driveway. He lost his job, his heart, and his hope. The neighbors cared for Albert over the years with polite invitations to holiday parties and birthday celebrations. A pie or basket of freshly baked cookies were constants on his front porch, but poor Albert was so full of grief that nothing could console his inner torment.

Albert finally found help with a clinic that treated men suffering from war trauma. He never drank or smoked and was reluctant to take medication, but given that he had lost everything, he figured he had nothing else to lose and started taking the pills, which subdued the demons and allowed Albert to deal with his suppressed horrors of the war. Then the unexpected, the impossible, happened: Elda came to visit after almost ten years.

The taxi, as he had imagined it would for so many years, pulled into the driveway and an older yet still pretty Elda emerged. She looked up at their once beautiful home and cried. Albert took her small hand and tenderly kissed her wedding finger that still wore his ring, and without a word led her to their porch swing and began to tell her of his regrets and his nightmares and about the help and understanding he had found through other veterans who also had shattered lives. He told her the terrible things he was forced to do in the war that didn't agree with his soul. His tender brown eyes blinked rapidly as if in disbelief that Elda was actually back, sitting before him. They talked all day until dusk, holding hands as they gently rocked on the swing. Together they watched the sun evaporate behind the rooftops, casting a warm bronze glow as it went down. It was as if they had just met, sharing thoughts and dreams of what still could be.

The house creaked and sighed as a gentle breeze blew through their grand porch. Dusk was always a peaceful time of day, Albert thought, as he carefully pulled Elda's crochet sweater around her exposed shoulder. Elda, too, had been alone all the years that passed, never forgetting her true love, anguished and paralyzed with regret for having left Albert in his time of need. She needed his forgiveness; she needed her husband.

Elda rested her head on Albert's shoulder as he assured her the nightmares had gone away for good, that they could still have their life together. Elda's broken heart filled up with so much love in that moment that it just gave out right then and there, on the porch swing, as she rested her head and watched the stars start to pop into the navy blue sky with her one and only true love. She saw a shooting star dust across the sky and she made a wish and closed her eyes and inhaled the fragrant twilight air. She slumped back onto Albert's shoulder and he just smiled and adjusted her throw over her lap. It took him an hour to realize she had left once again.

I remember the look on my mother's face when she asked me, while gathering the puppies together for feeding time, "Tutor, Sweetie, how would you feel about giving Mr. Albert Early a puppy? Maybe one of the sturdy male pups so he can at least go out for a walk with some company. He seems so desperately lonely and I think it would be a most kind thing to do." She wore one of my father's oversized sweaters. It was red and I knew it wasn't just Mr. Early she was thinking of. I had hoped this subject would disappear, but she couldn't let it go. "I'm just not sure which puppy would suit him," she said. They are still so young, and their personalities are too. But poor man, he's been alone for so many years . . . Anyway, it was just a thought." She gave one of her heavy sighs and I knew she had already made up her mind. She picked up a puppy and cradled it on its back. It was the size of her hand and she asked it if it would like to meet Mr. Early as it yawned and gazed up at her.

I looked at all the little wet noses pointing up at me and thought about Mr. Early. "A dinner invitation would be the perfect way to see which puppy takes a liking to him!" my mother triumphantly announced. I told her I was worried that none of the puppies would like him, that he was too old.

"Tutor!" she snapped, "that's not true at all. He's only about fifty and you're not being very compassionate. Mr. Early suffers from anguish—and that alone can age a person's soul." Feeling the sting of shame, I said I was sorry. "But," I still questioned, "Mr. Early will have to pass The Test, right Momo?" My cheeks were burning as she told me, "Yes, and he will."

***

The next afternoon after school, the three of us, with HoneyWest leading the way, as if she already knew what was about to happen, walked down the street toward Mr. Early's house. The neighborhood kids stopped their routines of coloring the sidewalks and sparing over a basketball game to watch. Momo rang the bell and corrected her posture. She smoothed her blouse and pushed up her sleeves. Her bracelets jingled as she grasped her hands behind her back. I picked up HoneyWest and shushed her as she growled at the crows that caw cawed from the front porch railing, and positioned myself slightly behind my mother. I couldn't stand the thought of one of our puppies having to live in a place like this and gave a last-minute plea to my mother to turn back home. But just then the door creaked slowly open.

The old man wasn't so old at all; in fact, he was very well-preserved and polite, but so disheveled. He greeted us in a whisper and glanced across the street to the kids who had stopped playing to focus on what we were doing. Momo graciously offered the invitation to dinner and he in turn humbly thanked Momo while running his hands through his messy, thinning hair. "Yes," he whispered, he would come for dinner the following night. My mother smiled broadly and said triumphantly, "See you then!" and took my shoulder to leave, which was a good idea since I stood frozen, staring up at Mr. Early, who was still in his pajamas.

My mother grinned and gave HoneyWest a nod and a wink and hummed all the way home. I, meanwhile, looked back over my shoulder, wishing the old house wasn't so awful. As Momo pulled me along, again I couldn't shake the thought of one of our puppies having to live in such a depressing environment, even if it would make Mr. Early not so lonely, and even if the puppy picked him.

That night, I sat on the back steps happily enjoying a Fudgesicle and admiring my lemon-colored Go-Go boots, which I only wore at home now. HoneyWest at my feet, I tried to imagine how Mr. Early felt being stuck in that sad old house with only ghosts and memories, and it made me cry. "A puppy would be the answer," I admitted to my faithful dog as I offered her a lick of my Fudgesicle. HoneyWest nudged her wet nose into my arm and squinted her tiny black almond eyes. She twitched her nose to the side and we both agreed that Momo was right as we headed to the puppy pen to see which puppy we thought might choose Mr. Early.

Nine

Crumpet

I carefully set the dining room table for three and admired my skill at setting such a fine table, something Momo had taught me when I was really little. She set the tables thoughtfully in her parents' small restaurant, she would tell me.

The "little details," her own mother had told her, made things all the more lovely. Momo always made everything look beautiful. Our house was almost entirely blue. "Wedgwood blue," Momo would say, with accents of color here and there. Every wall and all the carpeting were Wedgwood blue, too. It was calming and peaceful in our house with the antiques and modern mixed together. Yet all our furniture—the couch, the chairs, and the bedding—were white. Momo said the white reminded her of clouds. It was her heaven. In Momo's mind, heaven was blue with pretty details and big white clouds. The only completely masculine room in the house was Raleigh's den, filled with books and artifacts, framed magazine covers and photographs of Momo in beautiful settings. And, of course, his whiskey bar, the focal point of the room, was very large and made from rich cherry wood. Raleigh handcrafted the bar himself, Momo said. It displayed an array of unique bottles from all over the world, positioned perfectly on the glass shelves. The room was never used, only admired by my mother.

She would clip some roses and fresh rosemary from the garden, add a few sprigs of heather, and arrange them with great care into a few small vases, creating a soothing and inviting ambiance.

Mr. Early arrived spot on at six o'clock and nervously made polite conversation. He was shaved and dressed in a fine wool suit, and even brought some fresh sage that he hand-clipped for the very first time from "Elda's garden," he told us softly.

My mother was the perfect complement to his shyness, telling him her stories of Raleigh's photography, of the famous people he met on his photo shoots, and of his last assignment that went so terribly wrong. She told Mr. Early how she started to breed Yorkies, starting with the dog Raleigh had given her as a gift to lift her sprits shortly before he left.

Mr. Early opened up with each of Momo's stories, reflecting on his life long ago and his lovely wife, sharing a little about the war and its atrocities, but saying that losing his sweetheart was the worst thing he had ever gone through. War was easy next to that. There was something that kept him going, he said, and that was a feeling that he would meet Elda again someday. Because of this hope, he was able to sleep without the nightmares and instead had dreams filled with sweet stories of her, sweet dreams of his Elda.

The evening went well despite my early reservations, and with the pot roast and Yorkshire pudding nearly gone, the three of us sat full on food and storytelling. It was the perfect time for a piece of fig pie, and to bring in the puppies.

Mopsey's most recent litter had brought four little pups into our lives. These were the same puppies I'd shown my classmates and Scooter after school one day. At it turned out, this would be Mopsey's last litter, but we didn't know that at the time. She'd already decided that it was time for her to be left alone, without anymore puppies tugging on her for milk or following her everywhere she went. Mopsey would spend her later years with Butler by her side, and together they would lay in the warm afternoon sunlight, stretched out on top of our couch looking out the window; or maybe they'd go for a quiet walk with me and HoneyWest, or do what made them the most happy, catching gophers in our back yard.

In true Mopsey style, her last litter was a very interesting batch of pups. I called out to Mopsey, who was sleeping with her puppies in a large box filled with shredded newspaper in our laundry room. Butler stood at attention at once. Mopsey came quickly enough, yawning and stretching and wagging her tired tail as four black fur balls with shiny almond eyes trailed in behind her. Mr.

Early was clearly delighted. He put down his fork and set his napkin aside, clapped his hands together, and gasped out loud in amazement. "Oh my! Would you look at that!" he said, dabbing his eyes with his knuckle. They marched in like little black ants, bumping and tripping into each other, tails straight up like little antennas trying to navigate. We all laughed out loud as they lined up before us for review.

First there was Piper, a little male, the leader of the pack. Fiddle, another male and the timid one, watched from a distance; Bridget, a female who was never without kisses to give; and Crumpet, the runt female, a wispy little thing who possessed the most intelligent light brown eyes that always made me wonder what she was thinking. HoneyWest greeted the bunch of mops with a sniff and snort and then quickly cuddled into my lap, claiming me as her very own.

Mr. Early was beaming. He simply said, "May I?" and my mother said, "Please do," and very unexpectedly Mr. Early was sitting on our dining room floor with four puppies crawling all over him. Momo and I shared a nod at the pure happiness the puppies brought to Mr. Early. He rolled on that floor as a child would, in complete bliss. The pups licked his face, bit his ears, sniffed his hair, sat on his chest, barked at him, brought him toys, and demanded his full attention. Mr. Early was lost in puppy love, to say the least.

The night was a success, and when it was time to say good night, it happened again; it was the second time I witnessed it. Mr. Early was at our front door, raincoat on, hat in hand, ready to leave, thanking my mother for "a most enjoyable evening" when suddenly Crumpet appeared at the kitchen door. Momo saw her first, and quickly guided Mr. Early back inside to the living room couch for "just one more cup of tea," she pleaded. Mr. Early, not knowing what was going on, sat down with his coat still on. He took off his hat and slowly turned his head toward the kitchen. Crumpet, still peering out at us from the door jamb, slowly emerged and went straight to him, sat at his feet, and stared up at him.

She was smaller than his shoe, her fur just as black; her moist light brown eyes blinked and twinkled. Neither moved. They both just looked at each other for what seemed like forever and eternity. Mr. Early whispered ever so softly, "Elda?" And then he carefully picked up Crumpet. Her little tail wiggled as she meekly licked the tip of his nose and shut her eyes slowly. Momo and I pretended this was nothing special and both gave a nervous laugh. My heart raced and filled up with emotion. I gently took Crumpet from his shaking hands and back to the other pups as Momo grinned at Mr. Early and poured a little more tea.

After that night, Mr. Early came by three times in one week to visit Crumpet. "Clearly," Momo said, almost laughing, "our little girl Crumpet has found her new home, and I believe it's with Mr. Early." I knew it too, and we delivered Crumpet to Mr. Early when she was old enough, along with a warm bag of Yorkshire pudding.

***

Over the next few weeks, summertime started showing its arrival. The once vibrant green lawns flecked with golden brown and every flower seemed to buzz with a bumblebee. Anxious humming birds sucked up the last drops of sweet nectar and summer vacation plans were the main topic on the school bus. I would rush home after school to do my homework and, like always, watch the neighbor girls color the sidewalk with chalk while the boys showed off, popping wheelies down the street. I still thought they were odd. Everything was the same except this time Mr. Early was out front of his house with Crumpet in his arms waving a moving truck into his driveway. By mid-June, someone familiar was moving away and someone new was moving in. Change was indeed in the air.

I felt a tinge of excitement at the prospect of a family with lots of kids moving into Mr. Early's house, but I soon found out that it was the Donnerstag family, who already lived across the street from us, that was moving in, and that someone else, a woman with no family or pets, would be moving into the Donnerstag house. *No fun at all,* I thought.

Ten

HedyMae and Charles, 1937

Her name was HedyMae and she came into our lives in the early summer of 1969 to open her own restaurant, something not a lot of women—especially not a lot of black women—would have considered in the 1960s.

Long before the idea even came to her, though, she lived in Kentucky and met and fell in love with Charles Henry Riley, a big, strapping, red-headed Irishman who owned a small farm up the road—and on the right side of the tracks—from where she grew up and who frequented the coffee shop where she later worked. Charles was instantly taken with her exotic beauty and didn't know what to do about it. HedyMae was feisty with the male customers who craved her attention, but because of her coloring they never dared ask her out on a proper date. And so she refused to give Charles any attention, either, aside from a coffee refill. She considered him a big waste of her time.

He went to the coffee shop just about every day to drink coffee and eat pie, because no one in the world, he was sure, could make a pie like HedyMae. Her skin was like caramel-colored cream, her eyes light topaz. Her hair was too long and too curly and her figure was slim yet curvaceous. Charles smiled to himself at how people would whisper about her and how she kept her dignity no matter how they treated her. The owner of the coffee shop was hard on her, too, and had her doing just about everything that should have taken three people to do, but she didn't complain. She mopped the coffee shop floor every night at closing time, and then washed the dishes, took out the trash, counted the cash drawer, put the money in the safe, wiped down the chalkboard, and wrote the special pie for the next day.

She would go home exhausted. Every night she would pull her long hair up into a bun, wash her face, and look in the mirror and tell herself that someday things would get better. But each morning she started her life all over again, same as the day before. She got to work at the crack of dawn and got busy making the best pies in town for someone else's coffee shop.

That's how it all started. In the end, it was food that brought HedyMae and Charles together, and it was food that kept them together for almost thirty years.

***

Charles eventually got HedyMae's attention, as well as her heart. It just took a few years. His persistence was relentless and he didn't give a damn what anybody thought. Soon it was Charles who the locals whispered about, and he just smiled.

They were a young couple, in their twenties when they first met. Although they kept to themselves, they lived in a small town that didn't understand that love was colorblind, and going around town together was sometimes not worth the dirty looks. But neither one of them had ever left the small Kentucky town where they grew up, and they didn't know where they would go if they left, so they decided to take a huge risk, dirty looks and all.

The Depression had come and gone, and many people were in the position to spend money now, to experience things they hadn't had the chance to experience during those hard economic years. Together HedyMae and Charles created and opened a unique restaurant that embraced HedyMae's and Charles's fearless notion that food could bring different cultures together, no matter where you live.

During their early courtship, right up to their elopement, Charles and HedyMae would huddle together in a cozy corner of the public library and ruminate over picture books of wondrous countries, dreaming of all the places they would one day visit. They also spent time with cookbooks that contained recipes from places all over the world—some too fantastic to believe.

A small store became available in town, and it was perfect timing for their restaurant plans. Not too big, with a square room that had high ceilings and an enormous front window.

The kitchen appliances were all reconstructed by Charles himself from second-hand junkyard restaurant parts. All the mismatched Goodwill tables and chairs only added to the restaurant's unique charm. It had only ten tables, and a dozen large maps of the world were shellacked onto every inch of wall space. Much-needed candles, lots and lots of candles, to save on electricity, made the mood just right. They called their restaurant Travel Ho! Café.

Their plan was set. Charles would organize the books and keep track of the inventory. He would also greet the customers and wait on the tables while HedyMae would do the cooking. HedyMae was the creative force behind the recipes, while Charles grew the quality ingredients on their farm. But it was Charles Henry Riley, with his finely tuned taste buds and superb sense of smell, who gave HedyMae his final approval on all her dishes with a simple smile and a thumbs up. At the end of the night, they would count the money and wash the dishes together, side-by-side, gently swaying to the sweet sound of Billie Holiday that scratched from the old radio.

"THE WORLD AT YOUR MOUTH" the sign read, and just as she had at the coffee shop where she first met Charles, HedyMae worked herself to exhaustion. During the early morning hours, she would prep and bake while Charles got the restaurant ready for customers. He carefully set all the tables, polished the glasses and the cutlery, arranged the candles, turned on the music, and positioned the menu in the window.

People came in droves and the color of HedyMae's skin seemed not to matter anymore. The food was simply delightful and creative and not one person ever left without a full stomach and a good story.

Charles, often while waving a breadstick in the air, would relay fantastic stories of his and HedyMae's exotic travels around the world, telling tall tales about how their menu came about. He was the tester and the taster of all HedyMae's creations, he would boast, and as the years went on his girth was as large as his personality and his stories. No one ever knew that the two had never left their hometown.

TRAVEL HO! CAFÉ

MENU

RABBIT STEW W/CARAMELIZED BABY CARROTS
SAUTÉED FROG LEGS ON A BED OF DANDELIONS
BBQ BOAR SMOOTHENED RED APPLE SAUCE
ROAST GOOSE WITH GOOSE BERRY SAUCE
CRISPY EEL WITH SAUTÉED SEAWEED

SPECIAL DESSERT PIE OF THE DAY

As time rolled on, Travel Ho! became a town landmark. Regulars became parents and then grandparents, and on Sunday nights the line would wrap around the block as people waited for hours to enjoy this unique restaurant. After twenty-five years, a new restaurant moved to town and Charles got competitive; he decided their business needed to expand. They were not about to give up and had another idea: To build a chain of restaurants across the state.

Within a few years, tires grinded into the many parking lots of Travel Ho! Cafés. Business was booming and soon there were three cafés, then ten, then twenty, along with a lot of money. HedyMae and Charles, by that time in their late forties, sold the business for a fair fortune to a talented young chef who tried to change Travel Ho!'s concept, promptly ruining its uniqueness and running him right out of business. The chef ended up on television and became famous and wealthy anyway.

One by one, the restaurants closed down, while Charles studied a map in search of a much-needed extended vacation. "Fat as a stuffed piggy bank—yes we are!" Charles would chuckle but neither he nor HedyMae were truly happy. They missed the people and community who helped them flourish. Nothing pleased either of them quite so much as listening to people try to guess what exactly was in HedyMae's recipes. They traveled the world for years as they once imagined, and then did it again, until Charles announced he was tired and they at last came home.

HedyMae's boredom quickly set in, so she began to write down her thoughts for a new restaurant. She had another ingenious idea for bringing people together through her food. For months she ignored Charles and his recurring heart palpitations. He would stop whatever he was doing and grab his chest, catch his breath, and pull on the hand of whoever happened to be nearby, wanting them to feel the fluttering. It never hurt or caused him caution; he would just joke and say his heart was yearning for his HedyMae. Then, one evening, after a home-cooked test run meal—something that Charles had never had before, and which he loved instantly—he retired to the den to his favorite chair by the fireplace to settle in and hear all about the creation she had just made him. HedyMae knelt down and said she was ready to tell him about a new idea.

Charles removed his glasses and smiled at his wife. Her excitement filled his heart, even as it lightly fluttered, and he placed her hand on his chest.

"HedyMae, wifey of mine, you are the apple of my eye, my pie in the sky. I will love you, Sweetheart, until the day I . . . "

"Stop it, Charles!" she cried. "You are so theatrical!" And with that said, she pulled her hand away and leaned against his legs and began describing her next dream while Charles tilted his head to the side to envision it. He must have drifted off, just for a moment. HedyMae was lost in her idea and rambled on. Charles just smiled and listened, comfortably drifting in and out, stroking HedyMae's long curls. He was so relaxed, as if out on the placid ocean. He looked down at HedyMae with heavy lids and felt a flush of warmth on his face. He was admiring how the firelight glowed on his wife's beautiful skin, and off of her amber-colored hair. He whispered her name to make her look up at him. He wanted to see the light capture the gold in her eyes.

The light flickered on then off in that old coffee shop kitchen he remembered. It was so long ago when he first saw the exotic young woman who would become his wife. He smiled again at

HedyMae as she continued to describe to him their new restaurant. And then he remembered the neon light out front of the coffee shop where he would wait for her when she closed up. How it flickered and never worked quite right, and how he knew the moment he saw her that she would become his partner for life. That light had flickered and buzzed, just as their front porch light had in their very first home together, the house where he carried her over the threshold the morning after they married. He remembered that it buzzed with insects in the evenings—and the glow from the fire's flames strained his eyes and he rubbed his forehead and felt his chest. It was fluttering for HedyMae.

He remembered all the people who came to their restaurant. *It will be nice to visit with them again,* he thought. The old fluorescent light that hung in their first small kitchen buzzed, too. He would have to remember to fix that . . . The lamp light next to him was also too bright and started to flicker; Charles wanted to turn it off, but no need. Somehow it had turned off on its own.

Eleven

"Niche"

It took a long time for HedyMae to recover, and even longer for her creativity to return. Her best friend left her that night in the peaceful glow of the fireplace. Her idea was wonderful, he'd whispered. He'd softly run his fingers through her hair while she imagined out loud what they could create together again. A log shifted and sparks floated up the flue and Charles cleared his throat and gently rested his hand on her shoulder and she knew he had drifted off for a moment. She didn't mind, though, knowing that even in his sleep he could hear her.

Crackling, hissing, orange nuggets melted to cinder and down to ash as she fell asleep at his feet, head on his lap. She stayed that way until the next morning when the fireplace was as cold as Charles's hand that was still resting on her shoulder. Nothing could have prepared her for the next voyage she was about to take on her own, without Charles by her side.

She had been so excited about the idea of starting something new with Charles. They were such a good team. Together they had made their dream come true, despite people's doubts and reservations. Charles never mentioned the color of her skin—only that is was as soft as mink if anyone asked.

"Wifey of mine, maybe something a little simpler this time around?" he'd said to her just before drifting off.

She secluded herself for the first year after his death and grieved alone. She ended a lot of friendships with people she thought were her and Charles's dear friends—people who didn't understand her process of healing was solitude, or who didn't care to understand. It disturbed and disappointed her that her love and loss was not recognized like everyone else's love, and she didn't want to believe it was because of the color of her skin. She tried to travel a bit, but felt very lost doing so. However, along the way she did gather some new and old ideas. She reflected and mended and realized what she needed to do to feel whole again.

When at last she decided it was time to go home, back to where she grew up, back to the place where she wasn't accepted, is when she realized why she loved cooking. She was back in the place where she'd fallen in love with Charles, where she'd become the woman she was today, strong and steadfast, knowing exactly what she wanted: to create again a universally appreciated thing—great food.

It didn't matter who did the cooking as long as it was delicious, generous, satisfying, and thought-provoking. It had to make people want to talk about what they ate, and get to know the person who prepared it. It really was the best remedy for racial tension, and that's why HedyMae was passionate about her food.

That is when HedyMae knew she must move forward, and move she did—to California and our little Westside Village, just a few houses down from 432 West Denslow Avenue.

***

HedyMae came to check out the very modest and cozy little house that went up for sale on our street in 1969. She did not want to live grand. She wanted just a few things—a real fireplace, a reasonable kitchen, and a covered patio where she might cool a pie or two. She wanted to be able to watch the sunrise from her front window and to start a new life. She wanted to be able to hear the rain and thunder roar and not to be scared. She longed to feel something other than sadness. To not feel like half of her soul was missing. To remember Charles without the tears. What she yearned for was a simple little house to live the rest of her life in.

As it happened, the Donnerstags, who lived on our street, told Momo that Mr. Early was getting married. They already had their eye on his house—wanting more space for their several kids.

Yes, he was moving away and getting married to a lovely woman he'd met while walking Crumpet in the park one day. This woman, as it turned out, was also walking her little dog. Mr. Early and the woman were quite taken with each other, as were their dogs who, unbeknownst to them, were related.

They started meeting every day, sitting on a park bench and watching their two dogs play together like siblings. They would share stories of times past, of marriages and children, love and loneliness. And then one day, while feeding the pigeons in the park, Mr. Early accepted her dinner invitation, and she in turn accepted his marriage proposal several weeks later.

I remember watching Mr. Early on the day he moved away. He was whistling and smiling, looking years younger than he had when he'd been at our house for dinner. And there was Crumpet, right in his arms. A wave of happiness washed through me as a salty tear trickled into the corner of my upturned lip. And then I saw Mrs. Van Steenkiste's big shinny Cadillac pull up in front of Mr. Early's house. I wondered if Momo knew this was going to happen all along.

And so the Donnerstags moved into Mr. Early's house. With Mrs. Van Steenkiste's help and exceptional taste, he'd been able to restore the house to its original beauty in record time. He was happy to sell to such nice people with so many kids. Elda would have been happy, too. That was the plan he and Elda had, after all. A house to raise kids in. The Donnerstags were grateful for such an easy move—just three doors down. It was easy as pie, they said, and they put their small quaint cottage up for sale just around the time HedyMae came through town looking for a new beginning.

The day she moved in, June 15, 1969, my mother welcomed her warmly. Momo baked her some Yorkshire pudding, kept warm in a brown paper bag, and some homemade fig jam. The quiet, interesting-looking woman was taken by Momo's hospitality, and especially impressed with her unique Yorkshire pudding. I, on the other hand, had never seen anyone who looked like HedyMae before, and my ears buzzed from the talk that started circulating around the neighborhood about where she was from. Some people thought Jamaica, others thought Tahiti. Neither were places I had ever heard of before, but I imagined that Raleigh had probably been to both of them.

Momo told me not to listen to gossip, and when I asked if Raleigh had been to Tahiti or Jamaica she shook her head and knelt down to my level. She held my pointy chin firmly in her hand and looked me sternly in the eye. She said, "People from all over the world have different colors of skin, Sweetie, and what's most important in a person is their character, nothing else." With that she kissed the tip of my nose and told me she loved my freckles.

***

In the weeks that followed, HedyMae opened a restaurant in town—and not in the previous restaurant location that always had bad luck. Once again her idea was inventive, simple, and popular, and people stopped guessing about where she might be from. Her dinner pies were a delightful mystery, and, just as they had before, her recipes made for good conversation.

The neighborhood regarded her as "Chef HedyMae," and her tiny itsy bitty restaurant in the village quickly became popular for its unusual menu and its name: The Niche.

The location couldn't be beat. It was an old antique store on Main Street—a dingy narrow space that any passerby may have not noticed at first. Its small doorway was tucked off the street and the storefront had had a vacant sign in it for years. Only HedyMae saw its potential as a cozy little nook, and she quickly replaced the vacant sign with her own:

THE NICHE
PIE SERVED FROM 4 P.M. TO THE LAST PIE.

A little niche, she thought, on the main street. The decor was introspective, to say the least. The tables and chairs were all midnight maple and she placed simple midnight blue vases in the center, each one holding one small twig from an olive branch. The restaurant had Carmel-colored walls with a twelve-inch silver band that bordered the midnight blue ceiling. HedyMae would say it was her own her personal silver lining.

Her idea was brilliant, really. She offered one fruit pie a week for dessert, nothing else sweet. Her dinner pies, the main attraction, had hearty crusts and were full of exotic fillings and seasonings that caused quite a fuss. The dinner pies changed daily, and their ingredient combinations were endless. They came in all shapes and sizes, and no two pies were ever alike. HedyMae would make her pies at home in the early morning, let them cool down, just enough for the flavors to settle in, and then transfer them into her van for transport to the restaurant.

She made only fifty pies a day in the beginning, to see how they were received, and soon she hired some help and increased the amount to one hundred. No more than that, though. When the last pie was sold, the OPEN sign was turned over, and Chef HedyMae wore a satisfied grin on her face each time.

Twelve

Whiskey

Late that spring, after Mopsey's retirement, we'd decided it was time to breed HoneyWest for the first time. I had a hard time imagining her as a mother since she was my baby, but Momo assured me HoneyWest would make a fine mom and that she surely had more than enough love to give to me and her puppies. My mother always knew what my concerns really were. So we took her up north to meet a little male named Suitor, who was proud and sturdy, and from the moment they laid eyes on each other, we knew it was true love.

HoneyWest and Suitor touched noses and their little tails beat like hummingbirds and I knew that I now had to share my little dog. Suitor came home with us after that to live happily ever after. He simply could not live without HoneyWest, and his owner knew it— and so did I. Suitor entered our home after Crumpet had chosen Mr. Early and we were selling off the rest of Mopsey's last litter. He high-stepped through the house, around the yard, and up to my room, and HoneyWest followed. Suitor sniffed around and sat in the middle of the room and looked up at me, awaiting instruction. I sat down in front of him and told him what I expected of him. He listened intently, cocking his head from side to side, and when I was through, I scratched behind his ear and tapped the tip of his nose with my finger and told him, "Welcome home." It didn't take too long for Suitor to adjust. He sat on guard while HoneyWest slept and he let her eat first, and he always allowed her to lead the way. He would sulk when I took her for a bike ride without him, but he held vigil by the front screen door awaiting her return. It seemed to be a very good relationship.

Later, when HoneyWest became pregnant, everyone, Mopsey, Butler, and especially Suitor, were protective of her, never leaving her side while she waddled around the house unsure of what was about to happen. On the day it did happen, Momo was inexplicably nervous given how many deliveries she had assisted. But this time was different, and yet the same.

**

HoneyWest went into labor on my last day of fourth grade, or rather the first day of summer vacation. HoneyWest was hot, her temperature mirroring the thermometer on the outside porch. It blared one hundred degrees. She was scared, and so was my mother. You see, Mopsey was a big girl—almost twelve pounds, but Honey was only five. So when those puppies starting coming into the world, we were all surprised at just how many there were.

After the first puppy arrived, HoneyWest was wide-eyed, looking back and forth between us as the wet translucent black sacks came out of her. Momo gently, with her index finger, pushed away the smooth dark film from the puppy's nose and mouth as HoneyWest watched in fear.

Honey at last came to her senses and pushed her nose into her first born and started to lick it. A tiny squeak ensued and we were all relieved. The puppies kept coming while Suitor sat at the porch door on guard, howling to the moon like a wolf with each new offspring's yelp. Mopsey paced as Butler took intermittent laps of water and sniffed the air with each new arrival.

After the fifth puppy, HoneyWest was exhausted and slipping in and out of consciousness, but Momo knew one more puppy was still to come. Honey looked at me with such pleading eyes that I couldn't hold back my tears any longer and sobbed to my mother to please do something to help her.

HoneyWest was my dog, my girl, my best friend, my baby. I was frozen with fear.

All five puppies looked healthy—all about the same size, so Momo worried that the last puppy would be small and weak, unable to push its way out on its own.

My mother never panicked, but she also didn't look my way. Her skin was moist and pale and her hair fell from its bun in wet strands across her forehead. Her long fingers trembled slightly as she wiped beads of sweat from her upper lip. She kept calm and talked to the unborn puppy in a gentle whisper to "please come out" while she gently massaged Honey's belly, a gesture Honey was clearly grateful for.

Not soon enough, but thank God in the nick of time, the puppy emerged. Honey's feeble attempt to help remove the sack only upset me more. As I tried unsuccessfully to hold back my fear and my tears, I realized my only option was to hum. Otherwise I knew I'd get the hiccups, a reaction I got under extreme stress. So I hummed to my dog, something from a record Momo always played: "Moon River." Honey turned her gaze to me, her eyes glassy and half-open as her little tail slowly thumped against the shredded newspaper and box that we'd used to create a delivery space. I was grateful for her accompaniment because Audrey Hepburn I was not.

Momo respectfully removed the film, but the puppy lay still and silent, just like Honey was when she was born.

"Tutor!" My mother hissed, "go get the . . . " Without listening to further instruction, I ran to the kitchen just like before and got the amber honey. But Momo yelled out, "Not the honey! Go to the bar! This puppy needs something stronger!" I stumbled to the den, to my father's old bar that stood frozen in time. I stared at the bottles and the room began to spin.

My father loved whiskey, all kinds. He collected rare blends from all over the world, from all his travels. It was his passion and a hobby. Momo told me how a story came with each bottle he brought home. How I longed for him to tell me a story, any story.

I stood at the bar and was suddenly cemented to the floor. Within seconds my mother was behind me. She grabbed the first bottle off the bar and ran back to the puppy.

I watched her from the den with tunnel vision toward the kitchen as she hit her knees hard on the linoleum floor, then slid into the box, and with trembling hands poured a small amount of whiskey into the bottle cap. When she called for my help, I finally snapped out of my trance and came to her side. Numbly, I took the limp puppy she handed me and cradled it in my hands, on its back, as

Momo opened its mouth with her pinky finger and lightly put a drop of whiskey on its tongue and waited.

Momo's breath was the only sound, slow and heavy. I could see the puppy was a little male, perfect in every way, with a small gold tuft of hair on his chin.

Suitor whined while keeping a sharp eye on Honey's other puppies. He kept one ear twisted toward me and Momo the whole time we worked to bring the little puppy back to life.

The puppy's legs went stiff and the whiskey bubbled out his nose. I was completely horrified.

His tiny head arched backward and his tail went stiff and his nose turned pale. I yelled at my mother, "Stop it stop it! You're killing him!" In a harsh whisper she said, "Not this puppy." She gave him one more drop and he again arched backward. I was beside myself, hiccupping so hard I could have dropped him. Then he sneezed, three times. He relaxed and snorted whiskey foam out his tiny nose. Suitor sniffed the air and barked while HoneyWest, scared and exhausted, blinked her wet eyes that seemed to smile at me.

The puppy smacked his mouth as if enjoying the fine malt liquor and opened his blue-black eyes.

My mother, for the first time ever, cried over a puppy. She had learned long ago that to be in the business of dog breeding was indeed rewarding but also heartbreaking. She promised herself to let things happen naturally, not to interfere with nature, so this experience was something, just like HoneyWest's birth, I would never forget. With trembling hands she covered her mouth and let out a heavy sigh and shut her eyes until she regained her composure. Then she gave me a wink and a nod and I placed the puppy in her cupped hands.

For the longest few seconds they stared at each other, Momo's head moving in bird-like jerks as she regarded the little pup in her hands. He lay perfectly still, cradled on his back, looking contentedly at the human who saved his life. Then, all of a sudden, my mother let out a gasp. "Raleigh?" she said, and I knew it had happened again. I also knew at that moment it was okay to relieve my hiccups with a bite of lemon rind sprinkled with salt, a trick Momo said Raleigh had taught her.

We named the puppies that night as we sat with our family of dogs on the kitchen floor. Newton was the smart one since he came out first; Pudding the chubby one; Eva the beauty with her delicate features; Finny, the skinny one; Prudence, who had sound judgment enough not to be the last, Momo said with a laugh; and, of course, the runt, Whiskey, named after his life-saving elixir and after my father's favorite spirit. We had the honor of having Whiskey for almost twenty years. He was true to his breed and the most adventurous dog we ever had, and by all accounts he was my mother's dog and protector.

Whiskey was handsome and ended up being hardy, too, despite his precarious beginnings. He was not at all a Yorkie standard. He did not have long silky hair but coarse fur that was wiry and odd in color: he was blond. His legs were long, which made him taller than normal, and his stance was firm and solidly planted on the ground. His eyes were clear and intense and equal in size to his nose. Years later, when people came to the house to be interviewed to buy a puppy, Whiskey sat next to Momo sizing up potential owners. More times than not, potential buyers fled in discomfort due to his piercing stare. His eyes were blue.

Early on, still in his puppy stage, he claimed Raleigh's favorite chair and occasionally sat at the base of the bar and demanded, with his husky little bark, a taste of his life-saving malt. Momo never again spoke of the connection, but Whiskey was the man of the house and an expert gopher hunter, "Your father would have been proud of this dog." That much she did say.

Thirteen

Scooter Pie, Summer 1969

"You're growing up too fast," Momo often said, but always with a smile on her face and a kiss for the tip of my nose. She frequently marveled at the ways I entertained myself and at my creative instinct. Maybe because I was an only child I used solitude to conjure up strange ideas to pass the time.

That summer, one of my ideas was masterminding recipes to sell at my Sum More Stand. My tree house was the perfect spot for me to focus on my work. The first week the stand was open was a surprise. My strange assortment of goodies went over well. Even HedyMae said I had a talent for treats when she stopped by to see what I was selling.

Her kindness didn't change the way I saw her, though. She was something of an oddity to me. She was the only black person I'd ever known, and I perceived her as mysterious. Momo said not to judge her by the shade of her skin, but no one knew anything about her, and in our small community that in itself was very unusual. She came out of nowhere and she didn't have a husband or any family. All she had was her restaurant, Niche, that was the talk of the Village.

Her interest in what I was selling at my stand increased over the months, and she came by several more times to buy a few things. It became increasingly annoying to me, however, because I'd convinced myself that she intended to steal my recipes and use them in her restaurant. I needed to keep an eye on her.

***

Summer was in full swing and all the adventures I could imagine were waiting for me. My days were filled with the usual: an imaginary play, sometimes two performances in one day, starring myself, to be enjoyed by all the dogs that were held against their will in my cottage; or swimming in our pool, adorned in my mother's costume jewelry from head to toe, feet bound together sporting Momo's green rubber dish-washing gloves one on each foot, fantasizing I was a beautiful mermaid being hunted by toothless fisherman who were actually Butler and Suitor barking wildly at me as I sat on the floor of the pool looking up at them.

But riding my bike with HoneyWest in the front basket was the most fun for both of us. She'd point her nose into the wind and fearlessly lean into each turn I made I would pretend we were upon an unbridled white horse, running wildly though a forest of trees as a pack of black wolves snapped at its hocks. When I stopped and parked my bike with the kickstand, so I could run into the house for a Popsicle, HoneyWest would patiently stay in the basket and guard my bike until I returned.

My Sum More Stand was a smash hit that summer. It was the first time I was old enough to conduct business somewhat on my own. My confection stand was the talk of the town—though second to Niche—and I liked that people knew that my father had built it. In fact, I mentioned that every chance I got. I pretended I still had a father.

I felt a connection to Raleigh through the things he built for me. Every nail, every piece of wood, every detail was his craft. Sometimes I would sit in my tree house writing in the diary he left for me and I'd imagine what his laugh would have been like, or what he might have said about me on the day I was born. I missed him so desperately. I missed someone I never even knew. Raleigh's instructions on how to make change from a dollar bill and how to price my goodies according to their popularity came in very handy.

Twenty-five cents, ten cents, thirty-five cents . . . I was organized and thrifty and never ever gave anything away without a fair trade. Soon enough, Scooter Dubrow was hanging around at the stand almost every day. He was definitely impressed with my stand and my sweet popcorn and fast agreed to come over and help me collect the lizards that enjoyed sunbathing on our backyard wall in exchange for some free popcorn.

Yes, it was a bribe of sorts, but it worked, sort of, and Raleigh would have been proud of my bartering skills.

We competed, Scooter and I, in just about everything. We competed over who caught the most lizards, or who had the biggest guppy, or who could hold their breath longer in the pool, or who was the bravest in ding-dong ditch, or which of us had the most freckles. I beat him at everything. I did have the most freckles of anyone on earth, but I lost my confidence on the day I tried to count Scooter's freckles. When I glanced directly into his lime-green eyes, I was captivated, transformed. I was lovesick and I would never be the same.

As it turned out, Scooter Dubrow became my business partner that summer. "A business decision," I told Momo. She smiled and said, "Of course, sweetheart, Scooter will make a fine business partner." And then she smiled her pretty smile and gave me a wink. I hated when she thought she knew something about what I was thinking.

Scooter started helping me set up the Sum More Stand each day at noon. He mingled with the customers as a good manager should, ran the wagon to my house to get refills from Momo, which really helped our sales, and helped me close up shop at 3 p.m. Our plan was to save enough money to splurge on Disneyland at the end of summer. It would be so romantic, I blushed just thinking about it.

MY "SUM MORE" MENU

THE SWEET STUFF

PINK LEMONADE MIXED WITH GRAPE JUICE AND FROZEN BLUEBERRIES

POPCORN SPRINKLED WITH POWDERED SUGAR, CINNAMON, AND NUTMEG

APPLE KABOBS SLATHERED WITH CRUNCHY PEANUT BUTTER AND CHOCOLATE SPRINKLES

FROZEN BANANAS ROLLED IN OVALTINE AND RICE KRISPIES,
THEN CUT IN HALF AND SERVED ON A POPSICLE STICK

MELTED M&M'S SWIRLED INTO RAISIN BRAN,
THEN GENTLY MASHED INTO CUPCAKE TRAYS AND CHILLED

LUCKY CHARMS AND STRAWBERRY JELL-O LAYERED INTO ICECUBE TRAYS

NOT THE SWEET STUFF

VELVEETA CHEESE WITH A SLICE OF SWEET PICKLE,
WRAPPED IN BOLOGNA AND SKEWERED WITH A TOOTHPICK

BANANA SLICED AND SERVED ON BUTTERED SOURDOUGH BREAD
SPRINKLED WITH BROWN SUGAR

SPAM WEDGES SPEARED WITH BACON AND DRIED APRICOTS

LIVERWURST SPREAD ON TOASTED WONDER BREAD TOPPED WITH BOYSENBERRY JAM

I didn't know that all the fuss over my confection stand was what prompted HedyMae to stop by. The fact that she took notice of my knack for strange combinations, however, motivated me even more to expand on my creations and to stop being so annoyed by her. She was, after all, "brilliant," Momo said, at making outlandish dinner pies.

Momo and Scooter's mother went to HedyMae's restaurant on opening night while Scooter's big sisters, Wendy and Lolo, babysat me. I wanted them to be my big sisters, too. When Momo came home that night and couldn't stop talking about Niche, I felt a little competitive. I couldn't help but think HedyMae was up to something. However popular her restaurant turned out to be, she kept very much to herself, never socializing with the neighbors outside of her restaurant. Momo tried numerous times to have her over for tea, but she always politely declined.

"I need to keep an eye on her," I told Scooter, who just rolled his eyes at me. He just never understood anything. In my nine-year-old mind I was convinced boys just were not as perceptive as little girls. I surely didn't know that thought would hold true for a few more decades!

Fourteen

Pudding

By late summer, my mother was busy selling Honey's puppies, who were old enough for their new homes. She met many prospective buyers, though she turned most of them away. She knew the puppies would all eventually, sell as they were all so irresistible; only one would have a challenge finding the right buyer: Pudding, the fat little boy, was the one.

Short in his legs, as well as his back, he was compact and low to the ground. His coat was reddish and silver, which was strange, and his nose was larger than normal; his nostrils would flare with even the slightest shift in the air. His ears were small and very pointy and almost too close together, but they gave him an alert look, as if someone was calling him to dinner all the time. But it was his snuffling around like a hound dog that caused him, and us, the most trouble.

He just couldn't pick anyone to suit him as an owner, and with one sniff he generally walked away from any prospective buyers.

Very nice people from nice families desperately wanted to buy Pudding, but he was not interested. He just muddled and waddled and snuffled around the kitchen, cleaning up leftover piecrust and whatever else fell to the floor, growing larger and larger and less and less intent on going anywhere.

Momo seemed resigned to the fact that he had absolutely no interest in any other humans except us and that he'd most likely never be bought because of this, so she gave him all the love she had, just like anyone else in our little family of dogs.

***

For as much as Pudding seemed to not be going anywhere, during the summer of 1969, Momo, Mopsey, Butler, Honey, Suitor, and Scooter Dubrow were actually most busy putting up with me.

Daily summer events in my compact world, outside of my Sum More Stand, continued: climbing the tallest tree in our yard to listen to the neighborhood chatter and see some birds up close; swinging on my swing set as high as I could, standing up, with my eyes shut tight, feeling as if I were flying through the clouds. "Up Up and Away" was the song I would sing. It was a huge hit at the time and it was simply exhilarating to sing and swing.

Or I would spend hours catching pollywogs in a mason jar down the street at Miss Kimura's mossy lily pond. She had the most wonderful pond full of lilies and fish and bugs and life.

Miss Kimura was a soft-spoken woman and didn't mind me and Scooter fishing around in her lily pond. We would scoop our jars into the murky water and watch the moss settle and see who caught the most pollywogs. Sometimes we even caught a real frog!

I was completely fascinated at how the pollywogs turned into frogs, sprouting limbs and losing their tails. Scooter thought they were magical frogs. He was much cuter than he was intelligent. We were always sure to return the pollywogs back to their pond, never wanting to cause them harm. But somehow, some way, some would end up squished flat as a quarter in her driveway, no matter how diligent we were in our quest to deliver them back to where we'd gathered them from. They would hop all the way from the pond out to her driveway for some odd reason, like a death march. It was too weird.

"They are not magical," I finally told Scooter upon seeing one too many suicides. "They're just stupid!"

I liked catching sunbathing lizards off our back wall with Scooter while we enjoyed a cool watermelon Popsicle, as we didn't need to make trades anymore. But mostly I loved tending to the puppies. Honey had another litter and all of them had such different personalities, shapes, and sizes, and all of them had so much love to give. Their scruffy black coats and bald little tummies made them look like little monkeys, and they were just as playful and amusing. They would chase us, bite us, bark at us, and jump into our arms for more. And often, mid-play, they'd stop for a quick nap. And Scooter would softly pet them as they slept and smile so sweetly at them and at me. I think it was what I liked the most about him, his tender heart.

**

At almost three months old, Pudding was wider, his talent for finding food making itself apparent. He had quite an appetite and soon realized that there was better food than what happened to fall on our kitchen floor, or what Momo served up for the puppies' mushy meals. He fast found out just where the wonderful aroma that filled our quaint neighborhood was coming from.

He escaped more than once and was returned each time, in person, by HedyMae herself. And he would lick his chops and wag his stumpy tail every time. Pudding had developed a keen sense of smell and taste and he was fearless when it came to finding food. But cute as he was, it seemed not all right with HedyMae. Pudding, you see, had managed to dig his way under our fence, under our neighbor's fence, then their neighbor's fence, and their neighbor's fence, until finally popping up in HedyMae's backyard where her fruit pies sat cooling on her patio table.

She made those pies in the early morning hours, allowing them to cool before bringing them to Niche to be served as the daily special. Pudding was transfixed by her pies, and no matter how hard we tried to contain him, she brought him back home to us at least three times a week. And HedyMae was not happy about it at all.

The first time it happened she brought him back a dirty, filthy, scratched-up mess. He looked as if he'd been in a war. He'd dug all day long under four fence lines just to get to that aroma. But as his escapes increased, things like rose bushes, mean cats, watch dogs, angry gardeners, and even once our neighbor, who thought he was a giant rat, could not be avoided. Then, at last, he ruined poor

Miss Kimura's lily pond when he happened to fall into it while running from a hysterical HedyMae. He was a disaster.

I made it my mission to teach him to swim after he almost drowned in Miss Kimura's pond, which was only two-feet deep. I'd overheard a woman at the supermarket tell Momo how her Beagle had drowned in their swimming pool one afternoon that same summer, having not learned to swim and not knowing how to find his way to the steps.

That story so affected me I cried my heart out on the ride home, not knowing how to prevent this from ever happening to Pudding. My mother just smiled and gave me a wink and a nod and assured me that we could do something about it. While Momo put the groceries away, she told me to go put on my bathing suit and meet her at the pool. Perplexed, I did as I was told and hurried along with HoneyWest trotting at my heels.

Our pool had been fenced in to protect me when I was little. When I got there, Momo had unlatched it and let herself in. She was sitting on the edge of our kidney-bean pool, pants rolled up and a smile on her face. One by one she was joined by the pool's edge by Mopsey, Butler, Honey, Suitor, and Whiskey, who'd all come to watch the event while Pudding was busy licking the kitchen floor.

"Tutor, Sweetheart, when something makes you afraid, take thought and try to understand why. Then see what you can do to make the situation not so scary. I'll show you how. Now go get Pudding." With that, she stepped down onto the second step of the pool and pushed up her sleeves and took off her watch and bracelets. She was wearing very bright orange Capri pants with a lime-green silk blouse, and lots of long gold chains, one with a hanging purple nugget at the end. Raleigh gave her that one the night before he left and she wore it almost all the time.

When I returned with Pudding and a swim cap on to avoid green hair, she instructed me to lower him into the pool toward the deep end. Pudding was not happy, having never ventured near that end of our yard; the puppies were always contained in my playhouse area or inside our screened-in porch, so the pool was very foreign to the younger ones.

I did as she said and lowered him slowly into the water. I couldn't help but laugh at his reaction; he paddled the air as if he were swimming already, an instinctual reaction Momo said, but nonetheless ridiculous looking. Once he was in the pool, Momo instructed me to let go of him. And just as I feared, Pudding stopped paddling. Down he went like a brick. It all happened so fast, my scream, my mother diving into the water, my scream again. And then, up they both came, coughing up water.

Once he reached the step, Momo gave him a hard shove so that he catapulted onto the top step where he sat stunned, not even trying to get out of the water. Drenched to the bone, Momo sat next to him and grabbed his chin and looked into his eyes and told him it really was for his own good. And then we tried it again and again until I cried with frustration. "Stay there! Hold him for a minute!" she yelled. She marched to the house, soaking wet, and laughed out loud, "Sweetie, I have an idea."

I'll never forget what Momo looked like in that moment. Like one of my Barbie dolls taken into the bath for a little swim. Her black hair looked like glass it was so shiny and straight and her green eyes sparkled with excitement. It made me so proud that she was my mother, my Momo.

When she came back to the pool, she had something in her hand, and immediately Pudding's nose started to twitch. Back to the steps she went as she instructed me to lower him into the pool once again. I started to cry and to beg her to not make me, but she insisted. I almost dropped him because he started wiggling so hard, and as soon as he hit the water, away he went like a rocket! Straight to the steps where he was rewarded with a small taste of some food Momo held in her hand.

Pudding learned very quickly how to get to those steps no matter where he happened to be in or around the pool. "Pavlovian reinforcement," Momo beamed, hands on her hips. I didn't understand what she meant but whatever it was, it worked to help me know that Pudding would never drown. Neither of us could stop laughing.

Poor Pudding, by summer's end, was still hopelessly obsessed with HedyMae's pies, though. I was sure she'd cast a spell on him. No matter what we did or how we kept him locked up, he would escape and head straight to her back yard and devour her cooling pies. Momo said it wasn't just the pies that he was after, that it was more than that, but that we would have to wait and see what HedyMae decided to do about it.

Despite this, it was Miss Kimura who I really felt sorry for. All summer, on Pudding's jail breaks, he would plow through her lovely lily pond en route to HedyMae's and totally destroy it, and she never, ever once got upset. She would calmly smile and say, "Oh, that little dog of yours must have a sensational appetite!" And then she'd smile and scrunch her warm brown eyes and tell me it was okay. "He's just a little boy at heart, he means no harm."

Momo and I would always try to clean up the pond and leave her some Yorkshire pudding and a note with our utmost apologies, but there was never a response. She never got mad or upset, which prompted me to learn more about our sweet neighbor.

Fifteen

Miss Kimura

Miss Kimura's first name was Lily and she grew up in the house where I first discovered pollywogs. It was a tiny house, too small for the neighborhood. Her parents bought it in the midst of the Depression for almost nothing and turned it into a charming little cottage and converted the tool shed to a greenhouse.

Her father was the consummate gardener. Having first learned from his Japanese mother the art of perfecting the Bonsai, his talents evolved, as did his ambition. Soon, he was employed and well-loved by many for his extraordinary green thumb; he alone planted practically every tree on our street years before I was born.

When Lily was about twelve, she and her brothers started to help their father tend to his greenhouse and various gardening jobs in the neighborhood. She would rake and sweep, clip and trim, and plant seasonal flowers, while the boys mowed lawns and trimmed the trees. Soon her father had so many houses to garden that he decided to start a landscaping business. His wife, meanwhile, tended to the home and her beloved Orchids, a gift Lily's father had once courted her with.

The family stayed together in that house until Lily's older brothers left home in 1953, seeking adventure in the place the evening news was always talking about: The Korean War.

Her father was not happy with their choice. Having fled to America with his parents as a child, he couldn't understand why they wanted to go East. Opportunity was West! He wanted to groom them to take over the family business, but he had to settle for having his only daughter be the one to handle the books and billing. And then he placed an ad in the local paper for extra help for the harder work.

Lily was barely sixteen when she met a young man who came to the house looking for a job, having seen her father's ad. It was wartime and there weren't a lot of young men available to take on manual labor; the fact that he suffered from a twisted leg, a birth defect, meant he'd been turned away from the army. So Lily's father hired him on and he worked hard to prove himself to him—both to Lily's father, and clandestinely to Lily.

His name was Vincent. His nature was kind and Lily's mother was very fond of him, as he reminded her of her own husband as a young man. Finally, Vincent mustered up enough courage to ask Lily's mother for advice about what it would take to get her daughter's attention. She thought long and hard for many days and finally came up with an idea. She thought he should create something beautiful for her daughter—something that would last. Tulips and orchids and even roses were so common in Lily's everyday life as a gardener's daughter that he had to come up with something exceptional.

He pondered for weeks, trying to imagine something that would be as beautiful as Lily was, as lovely as her name.

One day he showed up with a shovel in hand and asked to build something for Lily right there in the back yard. It was clearly a labor of love. He put up a tent and worked under it, making sure Lily couldn't see his surprise. It took him one month to complete, and then he anticipated it would take on a life of its own with complete balance and harmony, just how he envisioned their future together.

Lily was more than astonished that the shy boy felt so strongly about her. As she watched him thump around under the enclosed tent she felt almost unworthy of such an enormous feat for the purposes of impressing a simple girl such as herself. But he'd taken to heart her mother's suggestion that the thing be "as sustainable as a good marriage."

So the shy boy with the twisted leg built Lily the most extraordinary lily pond there ever was, pollywogs and all.

***

Lily was only sixteen when the boy asked for her hand in marriage, and with both her parents' blessing and a promise to wait until she was eighteen, the two young people started their relationship and set their wedding date for the day after Lily's eighteenth birthday.

Their courtship was pure and honest and together they had a friendship first before ever so softly falling deeply in love. Lily and Vincent were undeniably kindred spirits. Each morning Vincent would arrive at the Kimura household, lunch box in hand, ready for his day's work. Mr. Kimura couldn't help but admire the young man's fortitude and began to feel as if he were his own son. He gave Vincent a lot of responsibility right from the start, partly to keep the boy's mind off Lily, but mostly to prepare him to understand the family business, as he most definitely would be his future son-in-law.

Vincent and Lily's sweetness together was something people talked about around our little village as they held hands across the table at the diner and smiled into each other's eyes, or snuggled at the Saturday matinee, giggling into each other's ears. While on his lunch breaks, Lily often joined Vincent on the cool shaded grass under their favorite Weeping Willow tree, where she would gently rub his twisted, aching leg, even though he never once complained about it. Vincent knew they were young for the ambitions he had, but he started planning their future by the end of their first year of dating when Lily's parents got word that her brothers would not be coming home—at least not for a very long time. One had taken a Korean wife and the other had achieved a higher rank and was staying on in the military. Mr. Kimura, ashamed at his sons' abandonment of the family, relied even more on Vincent, as he now would take over the family business without a doubt.

The two had a wedding date set and time moved forward. And then, with just one day to go before the happiest day of their lives, the boy with the crooked leg lost his not-so-good balance while trimming a very high tree. For Vincent, falling backwards from the ladder he stood on, looking upwards to the sky, through the leaves, hitting the branches as he descended, was not the painful part. It was the quick glimpse he caught in his mind's eye of Lily's future without him, and his knowledge, in those brief four seconds, that she would suffer.

Lily's father came home with the news and held his daughter for a long time, for he too was devastated for her loss. Lily never got over that young boy and never recovered from the moment when her father told her what had happened. She also never moved from that house, nor forward in her life. She never bothered anyone and was a quiet and sweet neighbor who didn't mind, and actually enjoyed, the company of children coming by to fish for pollywogs and frogs in her lily pond.

My mother had thought time and again to offer Miss Kimura a puppy for some company, but the right dog never showed up in any of the previous litters. We were hoping that Pudding, our little "left over" puppy, might be the one, but he was not about to leave us any time soon. We didn't realized it was fate once again having its say about which puppy was Miss Kimura's destiny. What Miss Lily Kimura needed was a "Beau."

Beau was a puppy from Honey's second litter, which came only a few months after the first. Born in late August, he was perfect, despite his slight defect.

***

Summer was over and my Sum More Stand was closed down till next year. Becoming a fifth-grader was on my mind, as was the arrival of Honey's second litter. Honey was once again very stressed during her delivery of the litter, and, as I mentioned before, she was small. Just as with her first litter, she held a whopping six puppies, one of which was Beau, crammed to the side, way in the back, up towards her spine. She slept a lot during the months she was pregnant, sleeping most likely to save up her energy for the arrival of her new puppies—and anything else that might occur.

All the puppies came out fairly easily to meet the Moot family, but little Beau did not. Just like Whiskey from the previous litter, he was the last one out. But unlike Whiskey, there was never a question that as to whether or not he would make it. He was upside down and backwards, scrappy and strong willed. His back left leg was twisted up into Honey's ribcage, causing it to twist like a corkscrew; but once all the puppies were out, Beau came right out too, as it was just a little cramped in there. I, of course, cried at the sight of him while Momo laughed out loud and clapped her hands, applauding HoneyWest. "Good job, little girl!" My mother held the little puppy up in the air and kissed his twisted leg and then pushed his cheek into hers and whispered, "Just in time, little boy! Miss Kimura will meet her new Beau after all!" I stared at my mother with amazement. How did she know such things?

Momo and I, when the time was right, delivered Beau to a very surprised Miss Kimura. She opened the door and stepped back, not sure of what we were about to do with the puppy I was holding. Momo assured her that it was our gift to her for everything she had put up with over the summer with Pudding repeatedly destroying her Lily pond. Miss Kimura was so polite that we didn't see that she was actually refusing our gift. She gently closed the door without us even realizing what had just happened.

My mother pushed up her sleeves and gave me a look and knocked again. Again, Miss Kimura opened the door and smiled sadly and said she really couldn't. It was far too much responsibility, and she'd never taken care of anything but plants and flowers before. A little puppy was just too much for her to handle.

Beau yawned at all the human conversation and we three stared at his sweet innocence and smiled. With that, Momo gently placed Beau down on Miss Kimura's doormat, at which point he stared up at her, yawned again, and stretched out his back leg, extending the corkscrew out to the side. Miss Kimura covered her mouth with a loud inhale and said, "Oh heavens!" She searched our eyes for some sort of understanding, but we stood our ground till it finally clicked.

It took another few seconds before she knelt down and introduced herself to her new Beau. She scooped him up and gently supported his twisted leg and brought him up to her mouth. She kissed his little head right between his eyes, and whispered something into his ear. His leg gave a slight kick, kind of a twitch in response to whatever she'd said, and then they seemed to smile at each other. Polite Miss Kimura forgot to say thank you as she softly shut the door in our faces, transfixed by her new puppy.

Momo and I stood there shocked at first, and then we began to laugh. We laced our fingers together and walked home with long happy strides, very pleased with ourselves.

Sixteen

Momo Knows Best

As love stories sometimes go, the "happily ever after" never happened as far as my father's return was concerned. That's what we thought before Whiskey came to us so unexpectedly, anyways. I was born in 1960, months after Raleigh toasted my conception and was gone forever. My mother suffered greatly but held on to the ray of light that was growing inside her.

My grandparents came to their daughter's aid and were there for my arrival. They cried with my mother when she announced that I would, without a doubt, be named Tutor, just as Raleigh had wanted. Momo and I survived just fine on our own, and together made a little life for ourselves and created our own kind of family with the help of our beloved Yorkshire terriers. And because of Momo, a lot of people over the years experienced their very own kismets because of our dogs and the connections they created.

About a year after I was born, my mother's headaches returned once in a while, and when they did, she succumbed to the darkness of her bedroom for days at a time, Mopsey and Butler by her side. She would sleep deeply and dream vividly and emerge fortified. Her doctor, who delivered me, always said it was a hormone imbalance, and that it had nothing to do with physic or clairvoyant abilities, which Momo chose not to believe. My mother had always known that there was something special about our dogs, she just couldn't articulate it. She knew why Mrs. Van Steenkiste kept Noble and why Mr. Early fell in love with Crumpet, and why we saved Whiskey. She determined that Beau, with his corkscrew leg, belonged with Miss Kimura too.

It was not until after Whiskey was born, however, that she finally surrendered and embraced her gift. My mother was convinced the moment she saw him, on the verge of being stillborn, that he was Raleigh in a dog's body. On nights after I'd gone to bed, she often walked past Raleigh's den to see Whiskey sitting in my father's favorite leather chair alone in the dark. Momo would go to him and sit across from him on the ottoman and hold his paw and make her own connection. Whiskey would point his nose toward the bar and then jerk back toward her, looking frustrated. She would pull him onto her lap and rock him and tell him, "I know," and he would give a heavy sigh and return to his chair, looking directly at the photo of her and Raleigh and then to the one of me, as a baby, that were placed on the table next to his chair.

Whiskey would always stare at my picture a long time and wag his tail slowly, pinning his ears tight to his head as if he had done something wrong. He then would sigh again and look up to Momo, peering into her soul, it seemed, with his piercing blue eyes. Her headaches would come and go, along with certain premonitions she experienced. Over the years she just learned to deal with the discomfort and the knowledge that what she experienced was more than migraines. She claimed to have a heightened sense of "things." Some things she would just "know," like how our puppies were supposed to be with certain owners, which continued for almost a decade. She said it was always up to the dog who its owner should be, but Momo had a hand in it too. I witnessed this my whole childhood—these introductions, the serendipitous moments, the perfect dog for a particular person.

***

My mother was compassionate and extremely sensitive, so her wanting to give away a puppy once in a while to a sad or lonely person made sense to me, but it was more than that to her. She had an acute intuition. She saw the bigger picture—which brings me back to the part of the story about HedyMae.

Around the same time my mother introduced Miss Kimura to Beau, with whom she indeed ended up falling in love with after all, HedyMae was still stubbornly refusing to surrender to her fate. After the experience with Miss Kimura, Momo became a bit frustrated at what she already knew was meant to be.

Pudding, our "left over" puppy, had been punished to the laundry room after his last escape. He was not allowed the same freedom as the other dogs and was put on a strict diet. My mother was perturbed—and not just with Pudding. HedyMae thought Pudding was overly persistent, and the way he stared right into her eyes bothered her. After he was rejected by HedyMae herself, his desire to escape seemed to wane, along with his appetite. He became severely depressed.

His mournful howling started into the second week of lock up and then Momo couldn't stand it anymore. "He's heartbroken!" she cried, with tears in her eyes. "That stupid woman just can't see it." So with Pudding under one arm and my hand in the other, she marched the two of us defiantly down our street one morning and pounded on HedyMae's door. When she answered, she seemed happy to see us—until she saw Pudding. Then her expression changed to something I can't explain.

At that point, my mother did something I couldn't believe. She actually got mad, furious in fact. "You fool!" she said. "Sometimes, if we're lucky, we get another chance to feel a connection to something or someone we have lost! I'm here to give you that chance!" And with that she handed Pudding to HedyMae and turned on her heel, grabbed my hand tight, and started walking back toward home. And then, without turning around, she yelled up to the sky, "Just open your heart, HedyMae!" She laced her fingers through mine and gave me a grin and said, "Let's skip home." She was once again the most beautiful mother in the world.

It was now fall, well into the new school year. We didn't hear from HedyMae, nor did she return Pudding after we left. My mother was pleased with her approach to HedyMae's stubbornness and chalked it up to another successful match on her part. Scooter and I were still catching lizards and pollywogs on the weekends and competing with each other about ideas for next summer's Sum More Stand menu.

We'd also set the date for Disneyland, a reward for our many months of good collaboration. Scooter and I were no longer in the same class, but it didn't matter, as we were the best of friends. The day at Disneyland was more romantic for me than it was for him, and ended early due to our exhaustion, as we went on almost every ride twice. Momo and Scooter's mother, Miss Texas, were our chaperons, and they decided to end the day and surprise us with dinner at Niche. The occasion ended up being one of those times in my life when I truly, utterly, down to my core, was ashamed of myself, which was something I hadn't experienced much up to that point in my life.

The mid-October sky was cotton candy pink and navy blue that night as we arrived at Niche. The anticipation of having a grown-up night and some really good food was almost better then Disneyland. Scooter and I on a real date, aside from our mothers being there, was my dream come true, and also well-earned after our summer of hard work. But thanks to my overactive imagination and my bad feelings for HedyMae, the special pie of the week sparked my worst fears that just so happened to be my worst nightmare.

I remember the chalkboard blaring:

TODAY'S SPECIAL
"YORKSHIRE PUDDING PIE"

My face went numb, my hands started to shake, and the room vibrated. And then I heard it, Momo's laughter, and Scooter pointing up to the chalkboard.

"Look mom!" he said.

"Well, isn't that creative?" Miss Texas responded in a slow drawl, while Momo stared at me, looking for my reaction.

The slow burning started deep in my throat, and then even a little vomit came up, followed by a shrill screech that exploded in my ears even though I was the one who screamed: *"Noooooooooo! Not Puuuuuddddddding!"*

The entire restaurant went silent, but that didn't stop me. "She killed Pudding! She killed our dog! I knew it! I knew it!" It was all such a blur, all in slow motion, and I could never have imagined the strength my mother possessed until that moment in which she gave one swift pull of my arm and sharply brought me back to reality. Before I knew it I was out on the curb out front, crying and shaking and yelling for her to *dooooo sooooomethinnnnng!* Scooter was out there, too, yelling at me: "Tutor stop! What do you mean? Who killed Pudding?" Miss Texas just shook her head with disappointment and put her hands over her son's ears.

A few concerned customers rushed out to see what the hell was going on and I screamed for them to get the police. "HedyMae cooked our Yorkie! He's the meat in the pie!" I balled and then I threw up.

With that, Momo sank to her heels and brought me to her waist and held me tight, "Oh Tutor, Sweetie, it was supposed to be a surprise. HedyMae used my recipe for Yorkshire pudding and made a special pie with it." She looked me square in the eyes: "It was a gift, Sweetheart, from HedyMae to us, for giving her Pudding, who she loves more than anything! Come on, let's go see him, he's with her right now in her office."

She pulled me to my feet, licked her thumb, and wiped the foam that had gathered at the corners of my mouth. "He won't leave her side, Tutor. Pudding picked HedyMae."

A crowd was now gathered around us whispering, pointing, laughing at me. Momo took a deep breath and smoothed her blouse. She fluffed her big black hair, laced her fingers through mine, pointed her chin up, and pulled me back into the restaurant. We walked straight through the kitchen to the office as everyone watched in silence. Except for Scooter, who was crying.

HedyMae, very clear on what had just happened, stood her ground, hands on her hips. Pudding was on her desk, eyes boring into me. He let out the most absurd snort. I ran to him, picking him up and squeezing him tight. He was fat and very happy and even at that moment had one "whale eye" looking toward HedyMae. I was so ashamed.

HedyMae approached me and knelt down, petting Pudding while she spoke. "My husband Charles would have loved this recipe—this Yorkshire pudding pie that your mother created special for your daddy. So just for tonight let's pretend they both are here with us and enjoy this special pie together. What do you say?"

I put down Pudding slowly and with a heavy heart apologized for my awful imagination and horrible behavior. My mother stood with her hands folded across her chest as HedyMae smiled and asked me if I had even noticed the special dessert that was listed on the chalkboard. I peered through the kitchen swinging door and looked up.

SPECIAL DESSERT
TUTOR'S AMAZING FROZEN BANANA PIE

I blinked and my eyes darted back and forth to everyone in the room, all of whom seemed to be glaring at me. My frozen bananas! She did steal a recipe from me after all! I was redeemed.

Seventeen

The Connections, June 2011

I swirl my glass of wine and admire its rich color and smell the orange blossom and lavender fragrances floating through the window. It was quite a time, that year of 1969. I felt things for the very first time in my child's heart, like distrust for Mrs. Van Steenkiste. She wasn't cold and unloving, just frozen in heartache—until she met Noble. I felt compassion, for Mr. Early. He was so sad and lonely—until he saw little Crumpet, and then he met Mrs. Van Steenkiste.

Then there was Miss Kimura, who I felt benevolent toward. I heard she had Beau for twenty years. She buried him alongside the lily pond in her back yard so he could remain close to her. There was Scooter, my first crush, who later gave me my first corsage the night he escorted me to our high school prom. And then there was HedyMae, whom I will never forget. I felt judgment toward her from the moment I saw her, but how wrong I was about her. She and Momo became the very best of friends, and ended up having a lot more in common than just making good food. They had both started their lives over for the very same reasons and went into partnership together for the next twenty years. HedyMae left her portion of the business to me when she died, and my mother and I were able to work together until Momo passed away, too.

Over the years and after so many doctors' visits, blood tests, X-rays, and everything else they could possible put my mother through, they never did figure out what the source of her headaches were. Cluster headaches, migraines, hormones, stress—all the hypotheses led to the same answer: nothing. Momo learned to live with the pain as well as the enlightenment that came with it. She would have an episode and retire to bed and a dark room for a few hours or days, depending on the severity, but afterwards she always felt a sense of "knowing," and whatever that thing was always came to pass within days of her feeling so awful.

Some believe she was clairvoyant or psychic and that she just didn't know how to handle it. I say she very much did—through her little dogs that carried their own messages from the afterlife. Not all of them did this, of course, but I surely remember quite a few.

Our Yorkies, Mopsey and Butler, who started it all; Whiskey and Pudding, who lived for one reason, to give Momo and HedyMae some peace of mind and understanding that love is, after all, transcendental. My beloved HoneyWest, my faithful companion, was eighteen when she decided that I would be just fine if she moved on. I miss her to this day and I feel her spirit often. In my mind's eye, her eyes still twinkle and look right back into mine.

Those were just a few of the ones that went straight to my soul, as if they were our guardians, Momo's and mine, to get us through the emptiness of losing a husband and never having had a father.

All of us that lived on Denslow Avenue during that time saw strange and wonderful things because of the Moot Yorkies, and I think, as of today, that half a dozen relatives of our original dog family still carry on with families from that time.

I know now that those puppies were a way for Momo to help me feel not so alone, the way she felt without Raleigh. Some people said she was confused by her headaches, that she imagined things out of the norm, but I knew my mother was never confused. Momo was very deliberate. I saw it, I remember it all.

***

Now, I look around my kitchen and smell the delicious blend of aromas that engulf it. Fragrances of orange blossom and lavender swirl around my head. I turn and lean back against the sink and smile at the five sweet faces looking up at me. I hold my wine glass up and toast to my father, and slowly start to come back to the present after a trip down memory lane.

My dogs would not stop staring at me, for however long my thoughts had taken me away. I give them a wink and tell them, "I know, I'm sorry, I sometimes reflect like that."

It was just one year ago tonight when my husband rushed to his client's house. I was in despair that evening, I realize now, and I didn't even know it. I was thinking about Momo and how old she would be if she were still alive, and how she would have loved my husband and thought my assortment of misfit dogs were adorable. I was missing her so much, and then, there my husband was. I didn't hear him close the front door; after all, he hadn't been gone long. I just saw the dogs wagging their tails out of the corner of my eye start, their eyes smiling. I remember turning fast to wrap my arms around my husband, feeling relief that he was home to shift my mind off my regret. But he stood in the doorway, arms held behind his back, overcoat still on. He always brought me flowers, and I thought what a perfect moment for them now. I needed a little something pretty to lift my spirits. I remembered him saying, "Tuts, I brought you home a little something."

I saw a black blur and then the dogs surrounding something on the floor. I shooed them all away and caught my breath. There she was, all two pounds of her, staring straight up from the tip of my bare foot. Her hair was already too long, covering her right eye slightly. She blinked her long-lashed almond eyes, and her tail vibrated like a hummingbird. She barked a raspy bark, too old-sounding for a puppy, and I laughed out loud. Our gang of dogs froze in anticipation, as did my sweet husband, for he already realized something special was about to happen.

He was explaining how his client's daughter was suffering from the loss of her mother, and that she didn't know how to process her grief and was acting out in anger. She was really messed up, he said, and had bought this little puppy not realizing that she couldn't possible take care of her. His client had asked if we wouldn't mind watching the puppy until he could find her a proper home for it. I laughed and kissed my husband for conjuring up such a story, but he insisted that it had happened exactly that way. I smiled as I admired the most exquisite canine jewel I had seen in a very long time.

I held my new baby in the air for a full examination as the other dogs sniffed and circled below. She was perfect. She was by far the most beautiful Yorkshire terrier I had ever seen. Her eyes were so bright and knowing, and she kept her gaze on me during the whole inspection. I looked at her teeth and inside her ears. I felt her knees and paws and tugged at her tail. She was sturdy and had the thickest, smoothest coat, as shiny as black glass. I was so completely enraptured with her that I stopped listening to what my husband was saying.

Finally, I stopped fussing with the puppy and carefully placed her on the floor for the other dogs to inspect. To my amazement, they all regarded her with the utmost respect. I looked at my husband and with a huge smile said, "At last!" I scooped my bundle up and started to ask her what name she would like when my husband spoke again, this time making himself heard. "Tutor, stop! Look at me! There's something very weird about this situation." I looked at him and saw that he was quite serious. I gave a tearful chuckle and said, "I know, you brought me home a Yorkie puppy because it's Momo's birthday today. You did remember."

I pushed the puppy's nose into mine and smelled the scent of sweet milk. My husband walked toward me and held me close. "Sweetheart, I didn't remember that, actually—I'm sorry. What I'm trying to tell you is ... my client's daughter has already named this puppy, and I find it more than a coincidence that her name is ... Monique."

As much as it gave me goose bumps in the moment, I changed my new Yorkie's name to Penelopie. I thought it fitting given the last three letters spelled "pie." She is my best friend, next to my husband, of course. Our other dogs fell in love with her right away, especially my little Chihuahua, Pixy Stix. I was worried at first because Pixy was my girl, my protector, and hated every dog that ever came near me. But she loved Penelopie, and treated her like her own puppy from the very beginning. Pixy would herd her through the house and bark at her to keep up. Pixy tolerated every bite and annoying thing she did, unlike my other dogs.

It was sudden, a few months after we got Penelopie, when Pixy had heart failure and we had to put her down. It was a changing of the guard, and one of the saddest days of my life. Pixy barked at the foot of our bed for weeks after she died. I knew this was not simply my imagination because Penelopie, who slept at the foot of our bed, would bark back.

My little Yorkie, who now never leaves my side, insisted on laying on my desk, right next to the computer, day after day, night after night as I wrote this story. She knows how important it is to me, to remember the good times, the good deeds, and all the kismets.

I have decided, upon much reflection, that people aren't so bad, as long as they have a kind heart and a good dog to help show them what unconditional love really is. HoneyWest and all the rest, I cherish the memories. Each of these stories hold a place in my heart, but the Yorkie, the Yorkshire terrier, holds a place in my soul.

The end ... for now.

About the Author

Stacy Erin Myers is the author and illustrator of *Maremaid: A Pony's Tale*. The inspiration for the story, about a coin-operated pony who wishes to become a real pony, came from having a horse of her own as a child—a beautiful Arabian mare, and her fixation on mermaids. After traveling to Europe with her mother at the age of five, Myers never forgot the magic and wonderment of the worlds most famous "little mermaid"—the sculpture in Copenhagen harbor.

Myers brought *Maremaid* to The L.A. Times Festival of Books, where it was noticed by Barnes & Noble. She was featured in The Los Angeles Times and later spoke to 500 third- to sixth-graders at local elementary schools about how to write and illustrate a story.

In addition to writing, Myers is an artist and a chef. Her oil and watercolor paintings have been displayed in local art shows and galleries. She launched "Stacy's Catering" in the early 2000s and ran that for several years before deciding to pursue her art fulltime.

In 2006, while working at home surrounded by her family of rescue dogs, she came up with an idea for another book. Having grown up as an only child with an eccentric Irish mother who bred Yorkshire terriers and loved to cook and a traveling businessman father who was rarely around, a story simmered in her heart. Always a believer in the hereafter, as well as serendipity, Myers conceived of Yorkshire Pudding.

Today Myers resides in southern California with her husband and one toy Fox terrier, two Chihuahuas, and one very special teacup Yorkshire terrier, all of whom are happy to sit at her feet while she creates a new dish or paints a new painting, or writes her next story.

www.ingramcontent.com/pod-product-compliance
Lightning Source LLC
Chambersburg PA
CBHW070503130626
46555CB00003B/1140